MARVEL CINEMATIC UNIVERSE
PHASE THREE

MARVEL

CIVIL WAR
CAPTAIN AMERICA

MARVEL CINEMATIC UNIVERSE
PHASE THREE

MARVEL

CIVIL WAR
CAPTAIN AMERICA

Adapted by ALEX IRVINE

Based on the screenplay by CHRISTOPHER MARKUS
& STEPHEN McFEELY

Produced by KEVIN FEIGE

Directed by ANTHONY and JOE RUSSO

LITTLE, BROWN AND COMPANY
New York   Boston

marvelkids.com

This book is a work of fiction. Names, characters, places, and incidents are the product of the author's imagination or are used fictitiously. Any resemblance to actual events, locales, or persons, living or dead, is coincidental.

Hachette Book Group supports the right to free expression and the value of copyright. The purpose of copyright is to encourage writers and artists to produce the creative works that enrich our culture.

The scanning, uploading, and distribution of this book without permission is a theft of the author's intellectual property. If you would like permission to use material from the book (other than for review purposes), please contact permissions@hbgusa.com. Thank you for your support of the author's rights.

Little, Brown and Company
Hachette Book Group
1290 Avenue of the Americas, New York, NY 10104
Visit us at lb-kids.com
marvelkids.com

First Edition: January 2017

Little, Brown and Company is a division of Hachette Book Group, Inc. The Little, Brown name and logo are trademarks of Hachette Book Group, Inc.

The publisher is not responsible for websites (or their content) that are not owned by the publisher.

Library of Congress Control Number: 2016952064

ISBNs: 978-0-316-27150-9 (hardcover), 978-0-316-31409-1 (ebook)

Printed in the United States of America

LSC-C

10 9 8 7 6 5 4 3 2 1

PROLOGUE

1991

Somewhere in the Soviet Union

A Soviet officer named Karpov punched the secret code into the keypad protecting a secure locker deep inside a remote base that did not appear on any map. The door opened, and he removed a small red book. It contained, among other top-secret information, the elaborate series of command words that would reactivate the experimental subject known as the Winter Soldier. This was only to be done for critical missions, but Karpov had just such a mission to complete. Only the legendary Winter Soldier could be trusted to do it.

As Karpov entered the laboratory, the Winter Soldier, barely conscious, was taken out of his stasis tube and brought into the laboratory. Soldiers locked him into a chair with a metal framework overhead, taking special care to secure his cybernetic arm. The containment divide dropped down to lock in place around his head. Karpov nodded at a technician, who activated large electrodes. Their crackle filled the room along with the Winter Soldier's screams. Karpov cared nothing for the Winter Soldier's pain. He only wanted a functional asset to execute the mission.

When the electrodes had finished their work, the Winter Soldier slumped, limp in the chair. Karpov opened the book and began to read in Russian. "Longing. Rusted. Seventeen. Daybreak. Furnace." Each word slotted into the Winter Soldier's head like a puzzle piece, slowly putting his mind back together. "Nine. Benign. Homecoming. One. Freight car."

The Winter Soldier raised his head, eyes focused.

"Good morning, soldier," Karpov said. He set the red book on a table near where the Winter Soldier, shackled and sweating, sat.

The Winter Soldier looked him in the eye. Did he remember that he had once been James Buchanan Barnes, best friend of Captain America? Could he? Karpov did not know and did not care. The important thing was what the Winter Soldier could do. The command words removed his willpower, and that was all that mattered.

"Ready to comply," the Winter Soldier said.

Karpov nodded. "I have a mission for you. Sanction and extract. No witnesses."

The Winter Soldier took his time observing the targets to establish their patterns. He chose the perfect night to execute the mission. When the moment came, he pursued the targets' vehicle, a stylish town car, down a remote country road. He shot out a front tire and the car crashed into a tree. Then he opened the trunk and found the object he'd been assigned to recover: a steel briefcase. He did not know what it contained, but that was not part of his mission. When he had secured the case, he made sure there would be no witnesses. The two people in the car would look as if they had died in the crash. The mission went precisely as planned.

When the Winter Soldier returned to base, the only thing Karpov said before scrambling his mind again was, "Well done, soldier."

CHAPTER 1

Present Day
Lagos, Nigeria

Wanda Maximoff was dressed in her street clothes, sipping coffee on the patio of a restaurant in downtown Lagos. As an Avenger, she was known as Scarlet Witch. She acted casual as she listened to Captain America's voice through a hidden earpiece. He was watching the area from an upper-floor window in a hotel down the block. "All right, what do you see?"

She looked around. The restaurant was across from the police station they were staking out. A pair of uniformed officers stood near the door. "Standard beat cops. Small station. Quiet street. It's a good target."

"There's an ATM in the south corner, which means—"

She knew exactly what it meant. "Cameras."

"Both cross streets are one-way?"

This didn't bother her. "So compromise the escape routes."

"Means our guy doesn't care about being seen," Cap said. "He isn't afraid to make a mess on the way out. You see that SUV halfway up the block?"

She did. "You mean the red one? It's cute."

"It's also bulletproof," said Natasha Romanoff, more famously known as Black Widow, who was sitting at a nearby table. Like Wanda, she was in a civilian disguise. "Which means private security, which means more guns, which means more headaches for somebody, probably us."

Wanda thought they were maybe worrying a little too much. "You guys know I can move things with my mind, right?"

"Looking over your shoulder needs to become second nature," Black Widow answered. She had a good reason to feel that way, and Wanda knew it.

From the top of a nearby office building, Sam Wilson,

code-named Falcon, chimed in. "Anybody ever tell you you're a little paranoid?"

"Not to my face. Why? Did you hear something?"

"Eyes on target, folks," Cap said, keeping them on mission. "It's the best lead we've had on Rumlow in six months. I don't want to lose him."

"If he sees us coming, there won't be a problem," Sam answered. "He kind of hates us."

They had been looking for Brock Rumlow since he'd been unmasked as a Hydra mole inside S.H.I.E.L.D., and they'd finally tracked him down here in Lagos. They suspected he was about to attack the police station, but they weren't certain yet.

Cap scanned the area and saw a loaded garbage truck forcing its way down a narrow side street, close to their stakeout location. As he watched, it crashed into a parked car, pushing it out of the way. Angry onlookers shouted at the driver, who ignored them. "Sam, see that garbage truck?" Cap said. "Take it."

Falcon touched a button on his armored forearm, and a bird-shaped robot took off from his back—he affectionately called it Redwing. It soared over the adjacent buildings and swooped down to street level, hovering under the truck. "Give me X-ray," Falcon said. Redwing returned a visual scan of the truck's interior directly to Falcon's goggles, along with images of the driver and data about the truck's cargo.

"The truck's loaded for max weight, and the driver's armed," he reported.

"It's a battering ram," Natasha said.

Cap realized she was right. "Go now," he barked.

"Why?" Wanda asked.

Cap was already moving. "He's not hitting the police."

The Avengers swung into action as the garbage truck accelerated out of the narrow street and across an open square in front of a research facility. A sign near the fortified gate read, INSTITUTE FOR INFECTIOUS DISEASES. The driver dove out and rolled along the pavement as the truck smashed into the gate, destroying it and crashing to a halt on the other side.

Two box trucks appeared from another side street, following the garbage truck's path. The institute's gate guards scrambled out of the way. A group of armed men in black body armor leaped from one of the trucks and shot their way across the parking lot, taking out all the security guards in the area. Then two of them fired gas grenades through the windows of the institute's main building.

As the gas took effect, the institute's staff dropped to the floor and lay unmoving. Masked and heavily armored men from the truck entered the building while the first combat team stood guard outside.

But they weren't counting on Captain America. He dropped over the institute's wall from a nearby building and disabled three soldiers before the rest knew he was there. From the top of a truck, he briefed the rest of the team. "Body armor. AR-15s. I make seven hostiles."

Falcon swooped low over an upper balcony overlooking the courtyard, spinning into a double kick that laid out two of the gunmen. "I make five," he said as Scarlet Witch arrived.

A gunman took aim at her, but she cast a swirling shield of chaos energy that no projectile could hope to penetrate. Then she caught him and flung him into the air, calling out, "Sam!"

Right on time, he dove down and smashed the flying gunman across the courtyard with the leading edge of his wing.

"Four," he said, and landed next to Cap and Wanda as Redwing scanned the building's upper windows. "Rumlow's on the third floor."

"Wanda," Cap said immediately, "just like we practiced."

"What about the gas?"

"Get it out," he said. The move they had practiced involved her using her powers to throw Cap across distances too far for him to jump. It worked to perfection. Red energy reached out to him and catapulted him up and through a third-floor window. He landed and knocked the nearest gunman sprawling, then ran farther into the building, looking for Rumlow.

Outside, Falcon deflected the incoming fire from Rumlow's men while Wanda used her powers to draw the gas out of the building. She built it into a tornado that spun up into the open air, dissipating where it wouldn't hurt anyone else. Remote-controlled mini-missiles from shoulder mounts on Falcon's armor took care of the closer gunmen, but there were still a lot of them.

Inside, Cap reached the secure lab where Rumlow had been. Shattered doorways and windows were an easy trail to follow. At the back of the lab was a cold-storage case with biohazard symbols inscribed on it. It was open and empty. Bad news. Turning back, he called to the team. "Rumlow has a biological weapon."

"I'm on it," Black Widow responded. She was on a motorcycle outside the compound, playing a support role and waiting for her moment to provide backup, and now she raced into the courtyard. She saw Rumlow in his battered metal mask, climbing up onto an armored truck to enter through its top hatch, but there were at least half a dozen armed men between him and her. *No problem*, she thought.

She laid the bike down and tumbled after it as it crashed into the first man. A second went down twitching when she hit him with her wrist-mounted electrical stingers. Three, four, and five caught boots or elbows to the face before they could get off a shot. Six dropped from another stinger, and then it was just her and Rumlow.

But he was a lot tougher than he'd been the last time she saw him. She hit him with almost everything she had, and he didn't stagger. She finally used a stinger, jabbing it straight into his neck, and he just paused long enough to say, "I don't work like that no more."

With that, he threw Natasha down into the armored vehicle…and dropped a grenade in after her. "Fire in the hole."

She had only seconds to act, but that was all she needed. With two quick attacks, she knocked out the soldiers in the Humvee with her. Then she crouched down, holding one of them in front of her to shield her from the explosion.

When the grenade went off, the blast blew Natasha through the Humvee's back door. She hit the ground and rolled to a stop, dazed for a moment. Then she saw where Rumlow was headed and called out to Falcon. "Sam, he's in the main Humvee heading north."

CHAPTER 2

Inside the truck, Brock Rumlow handed the crucial sample to one of his men. "Take this to the extract," he said, meaning the point where they would meet the buyer and leave Lagos. "We're not going to outrun him. Lose the truck."

"Where are you going to meet us?" the gunman asked. He stowed the sample in a duffel bag.

Rumlow's answer was grim. "I'm not."

Sam was in the air, soaring over the crowded streets. He saw the truck swerve and crash into a row of stalls at the edge of a market square. Four men spilled out the back of the truck and ran, trying to disappear into the crowd. Sam didn't see Rumlow. "I got four," he said. With the help of Redbird, he'd found them using facial-recognition software. "They're splitting up."

"I got the two on the left," Natasha said. She had "borrowed" another motorcycle and was swerving through traffic. She saw two men running ahead, but stalled cars blocked her path. Dumping the bike, she ran across the cars' hoods and wove through the crowd after them.

Cap reached the crashed Humvee a moment later and saw a vest and other equipment from Rumlow's men scattered around the street. "They ditched their gear," he said, scanning the area. Panic was spreading in the crowd, and he couldn't pick out the targets in the sea of running people. "It's a shell game now. One of them has the payload."

He made a guess where Rumlow's men had gone and had just set his feet to take off after them when he heard Rumlow himself call out from near the crashed Humvee. "There you are!"

At the same moment, a magnetized grenade clanked on to Cap's shield. Instantly, he threw the shield up into the air.

High over the square, the grenade exploded harmlessly, blasting Cap's shield away into the crowd.

"I've been waiting for this!" Rumlow growled. He charged forward at Cap, and the fight was on.

Sam tracked the two gunmen until they came out into an open space at the back of the market square. He swooped down and slammed into the lead man, plowing him into the ground. Then, getting a little extra lift from his extended wings, he spun and laid the other guy out with a double kick. Quickly, he rifled through their pockets. Nothing. "He doesn't have it. I'm empty," he reported.

Hearing that, Natasha ran harder, shouting at people to get out of her way. She caught up with the fleeing pair of Rumlow's gunmen in a side street lined with market stalls. Jumping over the nearest stall, she scattered its wares on the ground as she tackled the closest gunman. He went for his gun, but she held his arm and knocked the breath out of him with a flurry of gut punches. Then she spun toward the second man, closing in as she knocked the gun out of his hand with a heavy woven basket. She took him down hard, scissoring her legs around his neck and twisting him to the ground. His gun bounced free. Natasha went for it and came up, whirling around to see that the first man had his own weapon back. It was a standoff.

"Drop it," Rumlow's other man commanded from her left. Natasha leveled her gun. He was holding the vial stolen from inside the lab. "Or I'll drop this."

Natasha didn't know what was in that vial, but she knew Rumlow wouldn't have shot his way into the institute for something unless it was very, very dangerous. "Drop it!" Rumlow's man shouted again.

His partner looked as nervous as Natasha felt. "He'll do it!" he said.

Natasha hesitated. She couldn't let them escape with the vial. But what was the best way to ...

Sam solved the problem for her. His birdlike drone dipped into view and, with a single shot, dropped the gunman holding the vial. Natasha shot the other man in the arm and dove forward in a desperate lunge. That vial could not be allowed to hit the ground. At full stretch, she caught the vial inches from the ground and landed hard, clasping it and breathing a sigh of relief. "Payload secured," she said. "Thanks, Sam."

"Don't thank me," he said as he flew into view. He nodded at the drone hovering between them.

She shook her head. "I'm not thanking that thing."

"His name is Redwing," Sam said.

"I'm still not thanking it."

Catching up to them, Wanda looked at Redwing with a little smile. "He's cute," she said. Natasha rolled her eyes.

Cap had forced Rumlow to turn and fight, but this wasn't the same Brock Rumlow he'd known before. Rumlow had pneumatic gauntlets that gave him the power to hit like a truck, and he barely flinched at punches that would have put an ordinary man in the hospital.

"Come on!" Rumlow taunted him after knocking Cap flat and pounding him with a series of punches that left the Avenger bruised and staggered. He stomped the ground as Cap rolled away and got to his feet. He hit Cap again and forced him up against a wall. "This is for dropping a building on my face," Rumlow said. A blade snapped out from one of the gauntlets. Rumlow stabbed it at Cap's head, but the other man dodged and Rumlow's gauntlet buried itself wrist-deep in the wall. Cap grabbed the gauntlet and ripped it off. Rumlow raised his other hand, showing another blade. He swiped at Cap, who leaned back and used the motion to start a spinning kick that knocked Rumlow across the street, where he crashed into a patio table in front of a restaurant.

Cap knew Natasha had the biological sample. It was time to put Rumlow down and start figuring out what it was...and who Rumlow was stealing it for.

But Rumlow wasn't fighting back. He got to his knees and took off his helmet, showing his heavily scarred face. As Cap approached, Rumlow looked up at him, defiant and full of hate...but Cap could see sadness, too. And pain. "I think I look pretty good, all things considered," Rumlow said.

Cap didn't care to chat with Rumlow. Why had he quit? "Who's your buyer?" he asked.

"Your pal, your buddy. Bucky."

Cap wasn't sure what he'd expected, but he couldn't believe *that*. "What did you say?"

"He remembered you. I was there. He got all weepy about it—until they put his brain back in the blender. He wanted you to know something. He said to me, 'Please tell Rogers...when you gotta go, you gotta go.'" Rumlow's grin got bigger. He showed Cap a small detonator switch in his fist. "And you're coming with me."

Cap started to flinch back from the explosion as Rumlow

17

squeezed the switch, but then something incredible happened. Instead of blasting out to engulf Captain America and everyone else in the area, the explosion churned and rumbled around Rumlow. Cap saw the telltale wisps of red energy and looked back to see Wanda Maximoff with her hands outstretched. Scarlet Witch held the explosion's burst in check, her hands out and cupped in front of her. Then she lifted Rumlow and the fireball up into the sky, meaning to let it go off harmlessly.

But Rumlow's bomb was more powerful than she'd guessed. When she released it, the explosion tore through several floors of a nearby building. Smoke poured from the building's shattered windows, and debris fell into the street. The people who had been running from the battle now turned their shocked faces up to see what the Avengers had done.

This was bad. Instantly, Cap started trying to keep it from getting worse. "Sam, we need fire and rescue on the south side of the building." He ran to help. The last thing he saw was Wanda, looking up at the burning building with an expression of horror on her face.

CHAPTER 3

It was 1991. Tony Stark's mother, Maria, was singing and playing the piano. She stopped playing and looked over as Howard Stark pulled a blanket off Tony, who was stretched out on the couch. His parents had asked him to come home from MIT and watch the house for a weekend. "Wake up, dear. Say good-bye to your father."

"Who's the homeless person on the couch?" Howard cracked, holding up the blanket.

Tony got up and adjusted his Santa Claus hat, his way of displaying some holiday spirit. "This is why I love coming home for Christmas...right before you leave town," Tony shot back.

"Be nice, dear," his mother admonished. To Howard, she said, "He's been studying abroad."

Howard didn't seem impressed. "Do me a favor," he said, pulling the hat off and tossing it on the couch. "Try not to burn the house down before Monday."

Now standing, Tony nodded with mock seriousness. "Okay, so it's Monday. That is good to know. I will plan my poker party accordingly. Where are you going?"

"Your father's flying us to the Bahamas for a little get-away," his mother said.

"We might have to make a quick stop," Howard added.

"At the Pentagon, right?" Tony asked. He couldn't resist making a crack about his father's secret military business. "Don't worry. You're going to love the holiday menu at the commissary."

Howard looked at him, and Tony felt all the old conflicting feelings: love, resentment, and frustration. "You know, they say sarcasm is a metric for potential," Howard said. Tony turned his back and walked away to the other side of the room. "If that's true, you'll be a great man someday." He waited a beat, then turned to Tony's mother. "I'll get the bags."

"He does miss you when you are not here," Maria said

quietly to Tony, trying to lessen the tension. "And frankly, you're going to miss us. Because this is the last time we're all going to be together. You know what's about to happen. Say something. If you don't, you'll regret it."

She was right. Tony turned to his father and said the things he'd never been able to persuade himself to say in real life. "I love you, Dad. And I knew you did the best you could."

And then the adult Tony Stark appeared, observing the hologram projection of his younger self and his long-dead parents.

"That's how I *wished* it happened," he said. "By Barely Augmented Retro Framing, or BARF—I got to work on that acronym—an extremely costly method of hijacking the hippocampus to clear...traumatic memories."

Tony leaned on the piano. The hologram rippled and flickered into a jigsaw pattern of pixels. Then the Stark living room as it had been in 1991 was gone. He was standing in an auditorium at the Massachusetts Institute of Technology, where he was being honored as a famous graduate. The stage was just white cubes and a stand-in piano, to give the simulation some tactile reality. The emotional moment he'd just shown them...It had never happened. Not that way. It was all a simulation, and that was what he was there to talk about. He'd built the BARF system to re-create memories so people could experience them again and try to confront them by doing things they'd never been able to do in real life. It was a great piece of tech, but it wasn't making him feel any better.

"It doesn't change the fact that they never made it to the airport, or the things I did to avoid processing my grief," he said. Taking off his glasses, Tony looked out over the audience. They were hanging on his every word.

"Plus," he added, "six hundred and eleven million dollars for my little therapeutic experiment. No one in their right mind would've ever funded it. The challenges facing you are the greatest mankind has ever known," Tony said. They were silent, maybe hoping for some story about one of the Avengers' battles. But Tony wasn't here for that.

He shifted his weight, setting up for the speech's big finish. "Plus most of you are broke," he said, getting a small laugh. "Or rather, you were. As of this moment, every student has been made an equal recipient of the inaugural September Foundation Grant." A few gasps sounded from the crowd as certain people guessed what this meant. For the rest of them, Tony spelled it out. "As in, all of your projects have just been approved and funded."

The auditorium erupted in wild applause. Over the

pandemonium, Tony called out, "No strings. No taxes. Just...reframe the future."

Then he paused as the teleprompter showing his speech mentioned Pepper Potts. A shadow passed over his face, and he stopped following his prepared remarks. "Starting now," he said. "Go break some eggs."

He walked off the stage, leaving behind a lecture hall full of very happy students. The professor in charge of the event met him in the wings. "That, uh...that took my breath away, Tony. So generous, so much money. Out of curiosity...will any portion of that grant be made available to faculty? I know, gross, but hear me out. I have got this killer idea for a self-cooking hot dog. Basically, a chemical detonator embedded..."

Tony didn't want to hear it. Seeing Pepper's name had shocked him. "The restroom is this way, yeah?" he asked, pointing down the hall.

The professor nodded as an assistant strode up to him. "Mr. Stark, I am so sorry about the teleprompter. I didn't know Miss Potts had canceled. They didn't have time to fix it," she said.

"It's fine," Tony said, waving the apology away. "I'll be right back. We'll catch up later."

In the bathroom, Tony splashed some water on his face and looked in the mirror. He'd helped a lot of people today. That felt good. But the report from Lagos was heavy on his mind, and coming on top of losing Pepper...he was frazzled. Not that he could blame her. Not really. Tony had loved her, but she couldn't always rely on him, and both of them knew it. Now she was gone.

After Tony took a minute to get himself together, he headed for the elevator. In the hall outside the bathroom, a middle-aged woman was waiting for him. *A fan*, was his first thought. They were always finding him in unexpected places. "That was really sweet, what you did for the young people," she said.

"Oh, they deserve it," he said, and meant it. "Of course, it helps to ease my conscience."

She nodded. "They say there's a correlation between generosity and guilt. But you got the money. Break as many eggs as you like. Right?"

Tony wasn't sure what to say about this. He touched the elevator's call button. "Are you going up?"

"I'm right where I wanted to be," she said, and reached into her purse. Alarm bells went off in Tony's head, and he took a step forward to grab her wrist.

She didn't struggle. She just looked at him. "Okay, okay,"

he said, and stepped back again. "I'm sorry. It's an occupational hazard." The longer he worked with the Avengers, the more Tony had started to see threats everywhere. He was jumpy, overtired.

She slapped a photograph against his chest and held it there until he accepted it. "I work for the State Department. Human Resources. I know it's boring. But it enabled me to raise a son. I'm very proud of what he grew up to be." Tony felt a terrible sense of dread that he knew what she was about to say. "His name was Charlie Spencer," the woman went on. "You murdered him. In Sokovia. Not that it matters in the least to you. You think you fight for us. You just fight for yourself. Who's going to avenge my son, Stark?" she asked, pinning him with her angry gaze and leaning hard on the word *avenge*. "He's dead. And I blame you."

She walked away. Tony held the picture of Charlie Spencer. For one of the few times in his life, he had no idea what to say. Because no matter how he sliced it, Charlie Spencer's mother was right. The Avengers had killed her son.

CHAPTER 4

In one of the living areas of the Avengers headquarters, Steve Rogers, out of his Captain America uniform, watched news reports about the disaster in Lagos. "Eleven Wakandans were among those killed during a confrontation between the Avengers and a group of mercenaries in Lagos, Nigeria, last month. The traditionally reclusive Wakandans were on an outreach mission in Lagos when the attack occurred."

The camera cut to the Wakandan king, T'Chaka, speaking at a podium. "Our people's blood is spilled on foreign soil. Not only because of the actions of criminals, but by the indifference of those pledged to stop them. Victory at the expense of the innocent is no victory at all."

The announcer resumed speaking over video of T'Chaka and the burning building in Lagos. "The Wakandan king went on to—"

Steve turned off the TV and went into the next room, where Wanda was watching another channel on her own TV. "What legal authority does an enhanced individual like Wanda Maximoff have to operate in Nigeria?" a talking head was asking as part of a panel discussion.

Steve shut that one off, too. "It's my fault," Wanda said into the silence that followed.

"That's not true."

"Then turn the TV back on. They're being very specific."

"I should've grabbed that bomb," Steve said. He was the leader—it'd been his job. He sat next to her on the couch. "Rumlow said 'Bucky' and…all of a sudden, I was a sixteen-year-old kid again in Brooklyn. People died. It's on me."

She wasn't accepting that. He could tell. "It's on both of us," she said.

Steve had to remind himself that she was new to the dangerous business of being an Avenger. He'd fought a lot of

27

battles. She hadn't. "This job..." he said. "We try to save as many people as we can. Sometimes that doesn't mean everybody, but if we can't find a way to live with that, next time...maybe nobody gets saved."

Vision phased through the wall, interrupting them. Steve was always surprised to see him do that. The gem in his forehead gave him powers that none of them completely understood. Ultron might have tried to destroy humanity, but instead he created a new Avenger, and maybe the most powerful of them all. Those vast powers made a strange contrast with the way he dressed, like a middle-school history teacher. He liked V-neck sweaters.

Wanda looked up. There was a connection between them. Steve could see that clearly. "Vis, we talked about this."

"Yes," Vision acknowledged. "But the door was open, so I assumed..." He paused before going on. "Captain Rogers wished to know when Mr. Stark was arriving."

"Thank you. I'll be right down."

"I'll...use the door," Vision said, catching himself before he phased out through the wall again. He was still learning how his powers could make people a little uncomfortable. "Oh, and apparently, he's brought a guest."

"You know who it is?" Steve asked.

Vision paused at the door. "The secretary of state."

The current active Avengers—James Rhodes, Steve Rogers, Wanda Maximoff, Vision, Tony Stark, Sam Wilson, and Natasha Romanoff—sat at a long conference table as Secretary of State Thaddeus Ross paced while he decided how to begin a difficult conversation.

"Five years ago, I had a heart attack," the secretary said. He liked to frame his policy decisions with stories to put people at ease, especially when he expected people to resist the decision. "I dropped right in the middle of my backswing. Turned out, it was the best round of my life, because after thirteen hours of surgery and a triple bypass, I found something forty years in the army never taught me: perspective." He paused, the practiced politician giving his opening words a chance to sink in. "The world owes the Avengers an unpayable debt. You've fought for us. Protected us. Risked your lives. But while a great many people see you as heroes, there are some…who would prefer the word *vigilantes*."

"And what word would you use, Mr. Secretary?" Natasha asked.

"How about *dangerous*?" Ross shot back. "What would you

call a group of US-based, enhanced individuals who routinely ignore sovereign borders and inflict their will wherever they choose and who, frankly, seem unconcerned about what they leave behind them?" He had a remote control in his hand, and with those last words he started a video queued up on a display screen that took up most of one wall. Clips of the Avengers' most violent and desperate battles started to play as Secretary Ross listed the names of the cities that were being shown. "New York." Massive Chitauri creatures undulated through Midtown Manhattan, leaving destruction in their wakes. "Washington, DC." A burning Helicarrier plunged into the Potomac River. "Sokovia." Ultron's massive island, intended as a missile, rose into the sky. "Lagos." The wreckage of the burning building.

"Okay," Steve said. The Lagos footage hit Wanda especially hard. "That's enough."

"For the past four years, you operated with unlimited power and no supervision. That's an arrangement the governments of the world can no longer tolerate. But I think we have a solution." An aide handed him a bound sheaf of papers. "The Sokovia Accords. Approved by one hundred and seventeen countries. It states that the Avengers shall no longer be a private organization. Instead, they'll operate under the supervision of a United Nations panel, only when and if that panel deems it necessary."

"The Avengers were formed to make the world a safer place," Steve said. "I feel we've done that." He was trying to be respectful of the chain of command, but he also needed to be heard.

"Tell me, Captain," Ross said, "do you know where Thor and Banner are right now?" Steve didn't answer. He couldn't. Thor and the Hulk had been off on their own since the battle with Ultron. "If I misplaced a couple of thirty-megaton nukes, you can bet there'd be consequences. Compromise. Reassurance. That's how the world works." Looking around the room, Ross saw the resistance and hostility on the Avengers' faces. He decided to give them a little more context. "Believe me, this is the middle ground."

"So there are contingencies." Rhodey, speaking for the first time since they'd all sat down, didn't look happy.

"Three days from now, they meet in Vienna to ratify the accords." Ross gave them one last sweeping glance, making sure they understood the nature of the situation. "So talk it over."

Natasha asked the question they were all thinking. "And if we come to a decision you don't like?"

Ross had clearly prepared for that. "Then you retire," he said without hesitation. He left them to their thoughts.

CHAPTER 5

Soviet agent Karpov had escaped Russia a long time ago and hidden himself away in a new, anonymous life in Cleveland, Ohio. His past was his past. He didn't want any part of it anymore. But Karpov had worked deeply in top-secret operations, and he knew that he could never be truly free of it. He couldn't just start a new life. He had to destroy the old one.

Karpov couldn't quite bring himself to do that. He still kept some mementos of his work at the secret Winter Soldier base, and one of them was the red book. As long as he had it, no other person on Earth could activate the Winter Soldier.

Someone knocked at his door. "Hello?" a man called from outside. "Is this your car out front? I jumped the curb. Maybe we could take care of it ourselves." Karpov went to the door and listened, but he didn't answer. He didn't care about a dent in his car. His privacy was far more important. Let this fool worry about his own insurance company. "If you prefer to call the cops, then that's okay, too, I guess," the man said, sounding disappointed.

"No," Karpov said. He opened the door. "No cops."

On his doorstep, the man grinned. "Thank you."

But Karpov was completely unprepared for what came next.

He came back to his senses hanging upside down from his basement ceiling. His head dangled in the utility sink, where a trickle of water dripped down from the faucet. Karpov struggled a little, but he could tell right away that he wasn't going to be able to work himself free. The man who had tied him up was a professional. Better to talk his way out. It wasn't the first time he'd been in a dangerous spot.

Karpov watched as the man searched the basement.

Eventually, he found the aluminum box hidden deep in the wall. He dumped its contents onto a table near the stairs and spent a moment looking through Karpov's service files from decades ago. The red book containing the Winter Soldier's activation commands also fell out of the box. The intruder ignored it.

"You kept your looks, Colonel. Congratulations," the man said. Then he added, "Mission report: December sixteenth, 1991."

Karpov knew that date. He remembered the mission. How did this man know about it...and more important, why did he want that report?

"Who are you?" he asked, trying to buy time.

"My name is Zemo. I will repeat my question. Mission report: December sixteenth, 1991."

Keep him talking, Karpov thought. "How did you find me?"

Zemo relaxed. He picked up the red book. Karpov got a chill. If Zemo knew what the book contained...

"When S.H.I.E.L.D. fell," Zemo said, "Black Widow released Hydra files to the public. Millions of pages, much of it encrypted, not easy to decipher. But I have experience. And patience. A man can do anything if he has those."

"What do you want?"

"Mission report: December sixteenth, 1991." Zemo stood up. "Hydra deserves its place on the ash heap, so your death would not bother me." He sighed. Karpov couldn't tell whether his regret was real or not. "But I have to use this book, and other bloodier methods, to find what I need. I don't look forward to that."

Karpov knew this was the moment. If he told Zemo where to find the mission report, he might live.

But instead, all Karpov said was, "Hail Hydra."

CHAPTER 6

After Ross left, tensions among the Avengers didn't take long to come out into the open. The team was conflicted. None of them wanted to give up their ability to operate freely ... but that video montage had shaken them. Was there a better way? Rhodey and Sam staked out opposite positions right away.

"Secretary Ross has a Congressional Medal of Honor, which is one more than you have," Rhodey told Sam.

Sam wasn't impressed by the secretary's credentials. "So let's say we agree to this thing. How long is it gonna be before they LoJack us like a bunch of common criminals?"

"One hundred and seventeen countries want to sign

this," Rhodey countered. "One hundred and seventeen, Sam, and you're just like, 'No, it's cool.'"

"How long are you going to play both sides?" Sam demanded. Rhodey had been skeptical while Ross was in the room. Now he was taking the secretary's side, and Sam didn't like it.

"I have an equation," Vision announced.

"Oh, this will clear it up," Sam said, his sarcasm plain.

"In the eight years since Mr. Stark announced himself as Iron Man, the number of noted enhanced persons has grown exponentially," Vision said. "And during the same period, the number of potentially world-ending events has risen at a commensurate rate."

"Are you saying it's our fault?" Steve asked.

"I'm saying there may be a causality. Our very strength invites challenge. Challenge incites conflict. And conflict… breeds catastrophe. Oversight. Oversight is not an idea that could be dismissed out of hand."

"Boom," Rhodey said, leaning back in his chair.

"Tony, you're being uncharacteristically nonhyperverbal," Natasha said.

Steve had also been watching Tony, knowing that his opinion would sway people. "That's because he's already made up his mind," he said.

"Boy, you know me so well," Tony replied. "Actually, I'm nursing my electromagnetic headache. That's what's going on, Cap. It's just pain…discomfort." Restless, he got up and put some dishes in the common room sink. "Who's putting coffee grounds in the disposal? Am I running a bed-and-breakfast for a biker gang?"

Coming back to the table, he brought up an image on the wall display screen. It was the photograph he'd gotten from the angry mother in the hallway behind the MIT auditorium. "Oh, that's Charles Spencer by the way. He's a great kid. Computer engineering degree. Three-point-six GPA. Had a floor-level gig. A plan for the fall. But first he wanted to put a few miles on his soul before he parked it behind a desk. See the world, maybe be of service. Charlie didn't want to go to Vegas, which is what I would do. He didn't go to Paris or Amsterdam. Which sounds fun. He decided to spend his summer building sustainable housing for the poor. Guess where? Sokovia. He wanted to make a difference, I suppose. I mean, we won't *know*, because we dropped a building on him." Tony set his coffee cup on the table with a bang. "There's no decision-making process here. We need to be put in check. Whatever form that takes, I'm game. If we can't accept limitations, we're boundaryless; we're no better than the bad guys."

Steve could see why this was hard. He'd been there. He could conjure lots of faces of young men who didn't make it home from Europe. "Tony," he said, "someone dies on your watch, you don't give up."

"Who said we're giving up?" Tony countered.

"We are, if we're not taking responsibility for our actions. These documents just shift the blame."

"Sorry. Steve, that...that is dangerously arrogant," Rhodey interjected. "This is not the World Security Council; it's not S.H.I.E.L.D.; it's not Hydra."

"No, but it's run by people with agendas," Steve said. "And agendas change."

"That's good," Tony said. Clearly, he and Rhodey were on the same page. Steve wondered who would be on his side, if it actually came down to choosing sides. "That's why I'm here," Tony went on. "When I realized what my weapons were capable of in the wrong hands, I shut it down and stopped manufacturing them."

"Tony, you chose to do that." Steve was getting frustrated that Tony couldn't see the glaring problem with the accords. "If we sign these, we surrender our right to choose. What if this panel sends us somewhere we don't think we should go? What if it's somewhere we need to go, and they don't let us? We may not be perfect, but the safest hands are still our own."

He didn't have an answer to Steve's questions yet, but Tony could definitely see that Ross had given them a warning. Supervision was coming, one way or another. "If we don't do this now, it's going to be done to us later," he said. "That's a fact. That won't be pretty."

"You're saying they will come for me," Wanda said.

Vision tried to reassure her. "We will protect you." She didn't look convinced. To Steve's eye, she looked guilty and scared and ready for someone to tell her what to do.

"Maybe Tony is right," Natasha said. "If we have one hand on the wheel, we can still steer." Natasha knew even a year ago she would have thought differently, but things had changed since then. "I'm just…reading the terrain. We have made some very public mistakes. We need to win our trust back."

"I'm sorry," Tony said. He leaned on the table. "Did I just mishear you, or did you agree with me?"

"Oh, now I want to take it back," she said.

"No, no, no. You can't retract it. Thank you. I'm impressed by what you did." He stood and spoke to the group. "Okay, case closed. I win." Just like that, he was back to being flip Tony, the guy who always had a joke at hand. It was all so easy for him, Steve thought.

Steve's phone vibrated. He glanced at it and saw a text: *She's gone. In her sleep.*

The words were like a punch in the gut. Steve stared at them for a moment. Then he stood up. The rest of the conversation could wait. "I have to go," he said. Nobody tried to stop him.

CHAPTER 7

The choir sang a dirge as Peggy Carter's casket was carried into the London cathedral. Steve Rogers was the lead pallbearer on the right. He guided the casket to the front of the sanctuary, and the pallbearers set it down on a pedestal next to a large photo of Peggy and wreaths of flowers. A vicar, waiting in the pulpit, paused while everyone got to their seats, then welcomed them with a brief prayer. When he had finished, he said, "And now I would like to invite Sharon Carter to come up and say a few words."

Sharon reached the podium, and Sam, sitting on Steve's

right, nudged him. Steve had been looking down, lost in thought. Now he looked up and realized that he recognized Sharon Carter. She was the undercover S.H.I.E.L.D. agent who had revealed herself when the Winter Soldier shot Nick Fury in Steve's apartment two years before. She'd posed as his friendly neighbor to keep an eye on him at the time. How come nobody had told him she was related to Peggy?

Sharon took a moment to collect herself. "Margaret Carter was known to most as a founder of S.H.I.E.L.D.," she began. "But I just knew her as Aunt Peggy. She had a photograph in her office: Aunt Peggy standing next to JFK. As a kid, that was pretty cool. But it was a lot to live up to. Which is why I never told anyone we were related." She looked directly at Steve as she said that. "I asked her once how she managed to master diplomacy and espionage at a time when no one wanted to see a woman succeed at either. And she said, 'Compromise when you can. When you can't, don't. Even if everyone is telling you that something wrong is something right.'" She caught Steve's eye again, and he felt like she was speaking directly to him. "'Even if the whole world is telling you to move, it is your duty to plant yourself like a tree, look them in the eye, and say, "No...you move."'"

Steve waited for Sharon by himself in the beautiful stained-glass sanctuary. Natasha walked up to him. He was glad to see her, even though the question of the Sokovia Accords was the elephant in the room that neither of them wanted to talk about.

"When I came out of the ice, I thought everyone I'd known was gone," he said, looking at the photo of Peggy as he remembered her. Young, with beautiful dark hair swept up in a wave, gaze steady and strong. "When I found out that she was alive, I was just lucky to have her."

Natasha understood what he was getting at. She'd been torn out of her previous life, too. She'd had to leave people behind. "She had you back, too."

He was grateful to Natasha for taking a personal moment with him, but it was time to get down to business. "Who else signed it?" he asked. He already knew Natasha had.

"Tony, Rhodey, Vision," she said.

"Clint?"

"Says he's retired."

If Steve had a family, maybe he would do the same

thing, he thought. But seventy years on ice had put an end to that possibility. "Wanda?"

"TBD," Natasha said. *To be determined.* Steve wondered why Wanda was wavering, after what she'd done in Lagos. He wanted to ask about Banner and Thor, but he knew they were in the wind—*nobody* could ask them.

"I'm off to Vienna for the signing of the accords," she said. Natasha paused and added quietly, "There is plenty of room on the jet."

When he didn't answer, she kept trying. "Just because it's the path of least resistance doesn't mean it's the wrong path. Staying together is more important than how we stay together."

He couldn't agree with that. "What are we giving up to do it? Sorry, Nat. I can't sign it."

"I know," she said.

"Well, then. What are you doing here?"

"I didn't want you to be alone. Come here." They hugged. Steve wondered what it would be like if they ever really had to confront each other because of the accords. Natasha was wondering the same thing. Both of them knew what was coming, but both of them hoped it wouldn't be as bad as they feared.

CHAPTER 8

I n Vienna, one hundred and seventeen countries have come together to ratify the Sokovia Accords," a television reporter was saying as Natasha watched the delegates flow into the main meeting chamber and seat themselves. She was down near the front, close to the floor-to-ceiling windows that spanned the wall behind the podium.

"Excuse me, Miss Romanoff?" She turned to see a nervous bureaucrat. "I just need your signature."

Natasha signed the document without looking at it. "Thank you," the bureaucrat said, and melted away into the crowd.

"I suppose neither of us is used to the spotlight," said a voice nearby. She turned and saw the Wakandan prince, T'Challa. T'Chaka's son had his father's composure and bearing, but he was taller and...Natasha couldn't put her finger on it, but he seemed to radiate a self-assured confidence.

"Well," she said, "it's not always so flattering." The truth was, she hated spotlights and was uncomfortable with any attention she hadn't drawn to herself on purpose.

"You seem to be doing all right so far," T'Challa complimented her. "Considering your last trip to Capitol Hill, I wouldn't think you would be particularly comfortable in this company."

"Well, I'm not," she said. They were edging close to dangerous territory. Was he questioning her commitment to the accords? Were people going to be spying on them to make sure they did what they said they were going to do? Whatever it was, she didn't like the subtext of the conversation so far.

He got more serious. "That alone makes me glad you're here, Miss Romanoff."

"Why? You don't approve of all this?"

"The accords, yes. The politics, not really. Two people in a room can get more done than a hundred."

47

King T'Chaka appeared, inserting himself into the conversation with a joke. "Unless you need to move a piano."

T'Challa greeted his father. "Papa."

"Son." The king turned to Natasha. "Miss Romanoff."

"King T'Chaka. Please, allow me to apologize for what happened in Nigeria."

"Thank you," he said with a nod. "Thank you for agreeing to all this. I'm sad to hear that Captain Rogers will not be joining us today."

"Yes," she said. "So am I."

"Everyone, please be seated," the sergeant at arms called over the auditorium loudspeaker. "This assembly is now in session."

"That is the future calling," T'Challa said. He nodded at Natasha as she left to find her seat. "Such a pleasure."

T'Chaka turned to his son. "For a man who disapproves of diplomacy, you're getting quite good at it," the king observed, speaking Wakandan as they always did in their private conversations.

"I'm happy, Father," T'Challa said. T'Chaka patted his cheek, and T'Challa took his father's hand, kissing the ring that had been passed down from the ancient kings of Wakanda. At that moment, he was not a prince or a scientist. He was a dutiful son acknowledging his father's praise.

Once the assembly had convened, T'Chaka took the stage to deliver introductory remarks before the Sokovian Accords were officially signed. "When stolen Wakandan Vibranium was used to make a terrible weapon, we in Wakanda were forced to question our legacy. Those men and women killed in Nigeria were part of a goodwill mission from a country too long in the shadows. We will not, however, let misfortune drive us back. We will fight to improve the world we wish to join. I am grateful to the Avengers for supporting this initiative. Wakanda is proud to extend its hand in peace."

He was striking exactly the right note, T'Challa thought as he watched from the corner of the room near the windows. His father rarely exercised his diplomatic skills, but when he did, he usually got what he wanted. T'Challa himself didn't have the natural gifts of a diplomat. He had to work at it, and he preferred to spend his time almost anywhere else instead of in the conference room. His preferred subjects of study did not require he butter them up before they would work.

He gazed out the windows as his father went on speaking.

The assembly hall was on the third floor of the Vienna government complex, and he was looking down on a parked van across the street. Its rear doors were open and a pair of police officers were searching it. Standard protocol. Nothing unusual...until one of them stumbled back and ran away. The other did the same a moment later. He could hear their distant shouts and saw pedestrians start to scatter.

T'Challa instinctively knew what was coming next. The anonymous van, the sudden fear from the police... He sprinted away from the windows, toward the speaker's podium, shouting over his father's speech. "Everybody, get down!"

The words had barely left his mouth when the bomb in the van went off.

The blast caved in the building's front wall and turned the windows into a wave of shrapnel. T'Challa flew across the chamber and slammed hard into a support pillar. He got to his feet, ears ringing and blood on his face. Delegates screamed for help. Some fled and others were trying to aid the wounded. Frantically, T'Challa searched for his father. Fires were burning at the edges of the chamber, but he ignored them, fighting his way back toward the front of the room and the destroyed podium.

His father, the king, lay unmoving. T'Challa knelt at

his side, took his hand, and felt no pulse. Over the ringing in his ears, he heard sirens and screams. He smelled the smoke from the fires in the building and on the street. But none of it mattered. T'Challa crumpled over his father's body and cradled it, weeping at his loss...but already another fire was kindling inside him. He would avenge this. No matter how far he had to travel or who stood in his way, the king's murder would be avenged.

CHAPTER 9

After the funeral, Steve and Sharon went back to the hotel together and strolled through the lobby. He was enjoying the conversation, but he also wanted to know more about Sharon. She was a connection to Peggy he'd never known about. "My mom tried to talk me out of enlisting," Sharon was saying, with a wistful smile at the memory. "But not Aunt Peggy. She bought me my first knife holster."

"Very practical," Steve commented.

"And stylish," she added. They had reached the elevators and she pressed the UP button.

"They have you stationed over here now?"

She nodded. "In Berlin, Joint Terrorism Task Force."

"Right. Sounds fun."

She smiled. "I know, right?"

Before she went into her room and he lost his nerve, Steve had one more thing he needed to know. "I've been meaning to ask you. When you were spying on me from across the hall..."

"You mean when I was doing my job?" she said, gently correcting him.

Fair enough, Steve thought. "Did Peggy know?"

"She kept so many secrets. I didn't want her to have one from you." It was a hard thing for Steve to hear, but he understood. "Thanks for walking me back."

"Sure," Steve said. He paused, and so did she, like they both might have had something else to say.

But whatever it was, they didn't get a chance. Sam Wilson showed up then from the lobby, his face anxious. "Steve. There's something you got to see."

In Sharon's hotel room, Steve and Sam watched the shocking news. The government building in Vienna, its facade blown away and fires burning inside, dominated the TV screen. A British voice reported that a bomb hidden in a news van had partially destroyed the building.

Behind them, they heard Sharon talking with the Terrorism Task Force command center. "Who's coordinating?" she asked, and paused.

"More than seventy people have been injured," the broadcaster said. "At least twelve are dead, including Wakanda's King T'Chaka. Officials have released a video of a suspect, identified as James Buchanan Barnes, the Winter Soldier."

When Steve saw Bucky's picture, his first thought was, *No. That's impossible.*

Then he realized just how possible it was. "The infamous Hydra agent, linked to numerous acts of terrorism and political assassinations..." the broadcaster droned on.

How could Bucky have done this? Why would he do it? Why did Hydra care about Vienna?

Or was this an attack aimed at T'Chaka? Would Hydra go after Wakanda's Vibranium supply again?

Too many questions, not enough information. But Steve knew he had to find Bucky.

Sharon appeared between them, now off the phone. She watched with them for another moment and then said, "I have to go to work."

An emergency helicopter flew over Natasha as she found T'Challa sitting on a bench near the site of the explosion. Rescue and forensics personnel coordinated their response in a swirl of people around the devastated block.

She sat at the next bench over, facing him at an angle. There was blood on his clothes and dust in his hair. He had a heavy ring in his fingers, turning it over and over. She could see a pattern on the ring but couldn't quite tell what it was. "I'm very sorry," she said.

"In my culture, death is not the end. It's more of a... stepping-off point. You reach out with both hands, and Bast and Sekhmet—they lead you into the green veld, where you can run forever." He said it with a distant expression, his voice following the cadence of someone repeating a childhood story.

"That sounds very peaceful."

"My father thought so." He put the ring on and stood. "I am not my father."

Something about him seemed suddenly dangerous, and Natasha realized how little she knew about him. "T'Challa," she said, in case he had any crazy ideas, "the task force will decide who brings in Barnes."

"Don't bother, Miss Romanoff." T'Challa flexed his fingers, settling his father's ring into place. "I'll kill him myself."

As the grieving prince—now king—walked away, Natasha thought he was getting himself in way over his head if he believed he could take on the Winter Soldier. Her phone rang. It was Steve. "Are you all right?"

"Yeah, thanks. I got lucky." She looked around. Was Steve in Vienna? He'd been in London for Peggy Carter's funeral. "I know how much Barnes means to you. I really do," she said. "Stay at home. You'll only make this worse for all of us. Please."

"Are you saying you'll arrest me?"

"No. Someone will, if you interfere. That's how it works now."

"If he's this far gone, Nat...I should be the one to bring him in."

"Why?" This was no time for Steve Rogers to be working out his guilt, she thought. Things had gone way past that.

"Because I'm the one least likely to die trying."

He hung up then, and Natasha had two notions. One, Steve was probably right.

Two, a lot of other people would not agree.

There was going to be trouble.

CHAPTER 10

Steve was trying to look like just another American tourist in a baseball cap and aviator sunglasses when he met Sam at the counter of a coffee shop across town from the blast site. "Did she tell you to stay out of it?" Sam asked. He was dressed the same way. Steve didn't answer, so Sam added, "Might have a point."

"He'd do it for me," Steve said.

"In 1945, maybe. I just want to make sure we consider all our options. People who shoot at you usually wind up shooting at me."

Sharon joined them. "Tips have been pouring in since

the footage went public. Everybody thinks the Winter Soldier goes to their gym. Most of it is noise, except for this." She slid a folder over to Steve. "My boss expects a briefing, so ... that's all the answer you're going to get."

"Thank you."

She dropped some money on the counter to cover their drinks. "And you're going to have to hurry. We have orders to shoot on sight."

In a hotel room in Berlin, Zemo watched the news with the sound off. He had the red book open and was repeating the Winter Soldier command words. He wasn't a native Russian speaker, so he wanted to make sure that when the time came, he got them right.

There was a knock at the door. Quickly, Zemo hid the book and went to the door with one hand on his gun. "Herr Muller? *Ich habe Ihr Frühstück.*" *I have your breakfast.* It was room service.

He answered in German as he cracked open the door with a smile. "I could smell it before opening the door. Thank you."

"Bacon and black coffee," the hotel server said. "Again, I can fix you something different, if you like."

"It's okay. This is wonderful."

She was trained to bring the tray into a guest's room. "I'll put this on your—"

"No, no, no." Zemo took the tray from her. "It's okay. I can manage. Don't worry."

He thanked her and shut the door, relieved that she hadn't come in. There were things in this room that nobody could be permitted to see.

A thousand miles away, in Bucharest, Romania, Bucky Barnes was buying lunch at an open-air market. He had been on the run for two years, staying one step ahead of anyone who tried to find him. Bucharest was a good place to hide: big enough to blend in, but enough out of the way that he wouldn't accidentally run into someone he knew. Also, he spoke the language. He spoke a lot of languages. That had been part of his training. He remembered his training even though he didn't remember a lot of other things. He knew he was dangerous. He knew he had done some terrible things because terrible people had made him. He knew he didn't ever want to be controlled again.

He ate while he walked, with no special place to go. Nobody in the street paid him any attention, which was just the way he liked it. Suddenly, he got the feeling he was being watched. He had long ago learned to trust that feeling. Looking around, he saw a man in a street-side stall selling candy and magazines looking at him. Recognizing him. When the man saw Bucky looking back, he hung up a phone and disappeared.

Trying to keep his cool, Bucky walked up to the stall. There was a newspaper on the counter next to the cash register. He picked it up and saw his own picture under a headline claiming the Winter Soldier had set off a bomb at a huge government meeting in Vienna.

I didn't do that, Bucky thought. *I wasn't in Vienna.*

But someone thought he had. And that meant, sooner or later, they would track him to his apartment here in Bucharest.

Probably sooner.

Bucky got moving.

CHAPTER 11

Using the information from the file Sharon had given him, Steve found Bucky's apartment. He got in with no trouble and moved quietly through it, in full Captain America uniform and gripping his shield close. So this was where Bucky lived now. An ordinary place. Small, but ordinary. Steve started to search it, looking for hints about Bucky. Who was he now? Still the Winter Soldier? Bucky Barnes again? Or something in between? Brainwashing like Bucky's had long-term effects even after it was broken. He found a book on top of the refrigerator and opened it.

Looking back at him was a photograph of himself.

"Heads up, Cap," Sam said in his ear. He was standing lookout on a nearby rooftop. "German special forces approaching from the south."

"Understood." Steve felt a presence in the room with him and turned.

Bucky Barnes moved into the room, staring at Steve.

For a long moment, Steve wasn't sure what to say. He had more questions than he would ever be able to ask. Finally, he settled on one. "Do you know me?"

"You're Steve," Bucky said. "I read about you in a museum."

"They've set the perimeter," Sam said.

Steve put the book on the kitchen table. "I know you're nervous. And you have plenty of reason to be. But you're lying." The picture told him that Bucky remembered him, and not just from the museum.

"I wasn't in Vienna. I don't do that anymore."

Steve believed him, but he wanted to be sure. "They're entering the building," Sam warned. He was starting to sound tense.

"Well, the people who think you did are coming here now," Steve said to Bucky. "And they're not planning on taking you alive."

Bucky's voice was quiet. "That's smart. Good strategy."

"They're on the roof. I'm compromised." Now Sam sounded really worried.

"This doesn't have to end in a fight, Buck." Steve didn't want anyone to get hurt. Not Bucky, not the cops. They might have been the best counterterrorism force in recent memory, but they wouldn't be any match for the Winter Soldier.

Bucky looked down at his metal hand. "It always ends in a fight," he said sadly.

"Five seconds," Sam said.

"You pulled me from the river," Steve said. He could hear footsteps pounding on the building stairs. "Why?"

"I don't know," Bucky said.

"Three seconds!" Sam was shouting now.

"Yes, you do," Steve insisted. Bucky was scared—he could see that. He wasn't scared of Steve or any special forces team. He was scared of himself, because he knew what he could do. But Steve needed Bucky to see himself as a human being, not just the Winter Soldier.

Too late.

"Breach! Breach!"

As Sam called out that last warning, two flash-bang grenades crashed through the apartment's windows. Steve batted one back out the window with his shield. The other landed at Bucky's feet. He kicked it toward Steve, who

63

slammed his shield down over it. The explosion jarred his arm, but the shield contained it.

A split second later, the special forces team smashed in the front door. More of them swung in through the windows on rappelling lines, opening fire with submachine guns. Steve deflected the bullets and did his best to take the soldiers down without hurting them. Bucky went after them, too, hitting hard but not getting carried away just yet.

Still, after he'd slammed one soldier into the wall hard enough to cave in the drywall, Steve grabbed him and shouted, "Buck, stop! You're gonna kill someone."

Bucky pivoted and threw Steve to the floor. He drove his metal fist through the floor next to Steve's head...but then instead of throwing another punch, he pulled a hidden duffel bag from under the floor.

"I'm not gonna kill anyone," Bucky said. He threw the bag out his balcony door. It sailed over the railing. Steve couldn't see where it landed.

Steve was glad to see Bucky was keeping control. Together, they fought out onto the stairwell, where more special forces sprayed gunfire. All by himself, with Steve holding his rear guard against soldiers in the apartment, Bucky took down the whole squad in the stairwell. Steve came out to find a bruised soldier shouting into his radio that the subject had broken containment. He took the radio away and crushed it in his hand.

Bucky was a fighting machine, plowing through the soldiers as they tried to get up the stairs. Once, he got carried away and threw a soldier over the railing. Steve barely caught the man before he fell all the way down to the ground floor, fifteen levels down. "Come on," he said, frustrated. Bucky had to keep it together.

Bucky jumped over the railing, dropping several floors before catching himself on another railing with an impact that bent the metal into scrap. He swung up onto the landing and ran down the hall, building up speed. When he hit a balcony on that floor, he jumped all the way to the roof of a building across the street. He hit and rolled, scooping up his go bag in the same motion.

Steve was still working his way through the special forces team. He got clear and raced to the balcony just in time to see a black-clad figure come out of nowhere and send Bucky sprawling. Bucky got up just in time to ward off a series of strikes and slashes. Whoever the guy in black was, he was good. Fast and polished. He also had claws that cut through the metal pipes and housings on top of the building like they were paper.

Glancing up, Steve saw Sam vectoring in from his right. "Sam, southwest rooftop."

"Who's the other guy?" Sam wanted to know.

Steve backed up so he could build some speed to make the same jump Bucky had. "I'm about to find out." Sprinting forward, he hurdled the fifty-foot gap between the two buildings and got to his feet. The man in black had both clawed hands inches from Bucky's face. Bucky was barely holding him back with a heavy iron bar.

Then things got even more complicated. An attack helicopter swung into view and strafed the rooftop. Machine-gun bullets ricocheted off the black-suited figure as he stood tall in open defiance to the attack. Steve couldn't tell if anything had hit Bucky, but the shots had come awfully close to him.

"Sam," he said. He wasn't going to be able to dodge those bullets forever. Also, he didn't want Bucky to do anything drastic to the helicopter or the people in it.

"Got it." Sam vectored in behind the helicopter and knocked it off course the easiest way possible: by kicking its tail. It swung crazily away, its flight balance knocked off-kilter.

Bucky jumped from the roof, hit a ledge halfway down, and then jumped the rest of the way. He hit the ground running. The man in the black suit swung over the edge and slid down the wall, controlling his speed by scraping his claws along the side of the building. Steve leaped after him. The helicopter pilot had gotten the vehicle under control and started firing at Bucky again as he ran through the open square.

Weaving away from the gunfire, Bucky jumped down to a road cut below ground level, sprinting through traffic. The black suit followed him, with Steve hot on their trails.

Romanian police cars, lights and sirens blaring, caught up to Steve as they entered a long tunnel. "Stand down! Stand down!" the officers inside shouted over a loudspeaker.

Sorry, Steve thought. *No can do.* He jumped onto the hood of the closest police SUV. It screeched to a halt. He threw the driver out and punched the cracked windshield out of its frame. Then he squealed away after Bucky and his black-suited pursuer.

He passed the man in black, who made a flying leap and sank his claws into the back of the SUV. Steve sawed the wheel back and forth, trying to fling him off, but it didn't work.

"Sam, I can't shake this guy," he called out.

Sam answered immediately. "Right behind you."

Ahead of them, Bucky burst out of the tunnel and veered into oncoming traffic. A motorcycle sped toward him. With one hand he knocked the driver off, and with the other he held the bike, hauling it around in midair so by the time it touched the ground again he was going back the same way he'd started. On the way, he leaned down to grab his bag again.

The motorcycle roared into another tunnel, with Steve's commandeered SUV getting closer to Bucky. Bucky looked over his shoulder and threw a grenade up in the air. It attached itself to the edge of the overpass as he came out of the second tunnel. The grenade went off, and concrete debris cascaded down from the tunnel ceiling. The man in black hurdled the SUV's roof, braced himself on the hood, and leaped forward. Then, using passing traffic like a parkour artist, he jumped from car to car. With a final lunge, he caught Bucky and slashed the motorcycle's back wheel in half, throwing Bucky clear of the bike. Behind them, Steve saw the buckling overpass. He jumped out of the SUV and it hit the debris, rolling over and crashing into the median.

Steve was close enough to take on the man in black if he made another move at Bucky…but just like that, it seemed like every cop in Bucharest was surrounding them, guns leveled, shouting at them not to move. A moment later, War Machine dropped from the sky. He covered Cap and the man in black with repulsors at the ready. His shoulder-mounted cannon deployed and aimed at Bucky.

"Stand down," Rhodey said. "Now."

Cap wasn't going to fight Rhodey. Not now. He put his shield on his back and his hands in the air.

"Congratulations, Cap," Rhodey said bitterly. "You're a criminal."

The man in black raised his hands, too. He retracted the claws in his gloves. Sam had made his way out of the tunnel and was pushed into the group. The cops had caught him, too. Before they cuffed him, the man in black reached up and took off his helmet, revealing the face of T'Challa, the new king of Wakanda. Steve stared, amazed.

He hadn't known who to expect, but wasn't T'Challa a scientist, more lab rat than hardened warrior? Apparently not. He could fight, and that suit was superb tech. The Wakandans had a reputation for innovation, and it looked like it was all true.

"Your Highness," Rhodey said in surprise.

CHAPTER 12

In the kitchen of the Avengers compound he was sharing with Wanda, Vision was learning how to cook. At first, it seemed like basic chemistry: Put different materials together, apply heat. But now he was running into some confusion. "A pinch of paprika," he read from the recipe he had printed out. How much was a pinch?

"Is that paprikash?" Wanda asked as she came into the kitchen.

He nodded. She dipped a spoon into the pot and tasted the paprikash. "I thought it might…lift your spirits," Vision said.

She smiled at him. "Spirits lifted."

"In my defense, I haven't actually ever...eaten anything before, so..."

She understood what he was getting at. "May I?" she asked, nodding at the pot.

Vision stood aside to let her work. "Please."

For a minute or so, she busied herself with spices and stirring. "Wanda," Vision said.

"Hmm?"

"No one dislikes you, Wanda."

She looked up at him. "Thanks."

"Oh, you're welcome." He hadn't meant it as a reassurance, but it pleased Vision that she took it that way. "No. It's a...an involuntary response in their amygdala. They can't help but be afraid of you."

Holding his gaze, Wanda asked, "Are you?"

"My amygdala is synthetic, so..." He trailed off and she laughed.

"I used to think of myself one way," she said. "But after this, I am something else. And still me, I think. But... that's not what everyone else sees." She hadn't meant to get serious again, but that was where her thoughts were going all the time lately.

"Do you know—I don't know what this is." He touched the

gem in his forehead. "Not really. I know it's not of this world. But its true nature is a mystery. And yet, it is part of me."

Now he had her attention. Maybe they had this in common: Neither of them understood the true nature of their powers. "Are you afraid of it?" she asked.

"I wish to understand it," he said. Wanda wondered if he was afraid of anything. "The more I do, the less it controls me. One day—who knows?—I may even control it."

Yes, Wanda thought. *That is the goal.* She changed the subject after tasting the would-be paprikash one more time. "I don't know what's in this, but it is not paprika," she said. "I'm going to go to the store. I'll be back in twenty minutes."

"Alternatively, we could order a pizza?"

He had shifted in front of her as he spoke, and she realized that Vision wasn't just keeping her company. "Vision, are you not letting me leave?"

He didn't deny it. "It's a question of safety."

"I can protect myself."

"Not yours. Mr. Stark would like to avoid the possibility of another public incident. Until the accords are on a more secure foundation."

Ah, she thought. *Stark is handling the public relations for the accords, and he doesn't want anyone to see Scarlet Witch and remember Lagos.* That was why they were at his secure compound while the conversations that affected their lives took place thousands of miles away.

"And what do you want?" she asked. She found herself looking away from his earnest gaze.

"For people to see you...as I do."

And then, silence.

CHAPTER 13

A quick flight found the three men in custody in the back of a police van taking them through Berlin. Sam and Steve sat together, facing T'Challa. Steve didn't know where Bucky was. None of them had said anything yet. "So, you like cats?" Sam said out of the blue.

"Sam…" Steve said. He understood Sam's curiosity—and anger—but this wasn't the time. Why provoke him?

"What?" Sam shot back. "Dude shows up dressed like a cat, and you don't want to know more?"

Steve gave up. He was curious, too—he had to admit that. And after all, the fight had put them and T'Challa on the same side in the eyes of those who had signed the Sokovia Accords. "Your suit," he said to T'Challa. "Vibranium?"

"The Black Panther has been the protector of Wakanda for generations," T'Challa said, ignoring the question. "A mantle passed from warrior to warrior. And now because your friend murdered my father, I also wear the mantle of king. So I ask you, as both warrior and king, how long do you think you can keep your friend safe from me?"

They didn't say much after that. Steve was thinking about what Vision had said after the meeting with Secretary Ross; here was another enhanced individual they hadn't known about. But was he going to be a friend or an enemy?

After passing down a ramp somewhere in downtown Berlin, they were processed into an underground facility. There, Steve saw Bucky, manacled inside a sealed capsule, reinforced with who-knew-what kind of metals. He was being transported, and Steve wanted to know where. He spotted Sharon and was glad for a friendly face. "What's going to happen?" he asked, nodding in Bucky's direction.

"The same thing that ought to happen to you," said a trim, middle-aged man in a gray suit standing next to her.

Classic bureaucrat, Steve thought. "Psychological evaluation and extradition."

"This is Everett Ross," Sharon said. "Deputy task-force commander."

"What about a lawyer?" Steve asked. He didn't like the look of Ross right off the bat.

"Lawyer. That's funny." Ross held Steve's glance for a moment, then turned to Sharon. "See that their weapons are placed in the lockup." Looking back to Steve and Sam, he added, "Oh, we'll write you a receipt."

Sam didn't look convinced. "I better not look out the window and see anybody flying around in that."

Ross escorted them upstairs and over a pedestrian bridge, flanked by Sharon and Natasha. "You will be provided with an office instead of a cell," he said to the three rogue heroes. "And do me a favor. Stay in it."

"I'm not intending on going anywhere," T'Challa said evenly. Neither Steve nor Sam had anything to add.

Natasha fell into step next to Steve. "For the record," she said quietly, "this is what making things worse looks like."

"He's alive," Steve said. That was what mattered.

She clearly didn't feel the same way. Neither did Tony, who passed by long enough to say, "Colonel Rhodes is supervising the cleanup. Try not to break anything while we fix this." Natasha walked ahead of them. Steve and Sam exchanged a look as she went. This was trouble...but they knew they had done the right thing.

They caught up with Tony a few minutes later in a temporary office space. He was on the phone. "Consequences? You bet there will be consequences." He paused. "Obviously, you can quote me on that, because I just said it. Anything else? Thank you, sir." He hung up.

"Consequences?" Steve said. "For who?"

"Secretary Ross wants you both prosecuted. I have to give him something."

"I'm not getting that shield back, am I?"

"Technically, it's the government's property," Natasha said. She nodded at Sam. "Wings, too."

"That's cold," Sam said.

Tony shrugged. "Warmer than jail." He and Natasha walked away, leaving Steve and Sam in their so-called office space.

A while later, Steve stood watching a video feed of Bucky's armored cell being locked in to place on another level. He was in a command center with screens showing activity in every part of the station. Tony entered and walked up to him. "Hey, you want to see something cool? I pulled something from Dad's archives."

He showed Steve a set of pens. "FDR signed the Lend-Lease bills with these in 1941. Provided support to the Allies when they needed it most."

"Some would say it brought our country closer to war." Steve didn't feel like hearing Tony's stories.

"See, if not for these, you wouldn't be here. I'm trying to—what do you call it?" He searched for the right word.

Steve knew what Tony was trying to do. Hand him a pen, talk about important papers people had signed . . . but no. He wasn't going to sign the accords. "Is Pepper here?" he asked to change the subject. "I didn't see her."

Tony looked away. "We are . . . kind of . . . well, not kind of . . ."

"Pregnant?" Steve prompted.

"No, definitely not. We're taking a break. It's nobody's fault."

Oh, Steve thought. *That explained a lot.* Tony never told anyone about emotional things, so when he acted squirrelly, it was hard to understand why. But if he and Pepper . . .

"So sorry, Tony," he said. "I didn't know."

"A few years ago, I almost lost her, so I trashed all my suits," Tony said. "Then we had to muck up Hydra. And then Ultron—my fault. And then, and then, and then . . . I never stopped. 'Cause the truth is I don't want to stop. I don't want to lose her. I thought maybe the accords could split the difference. In her defense, I'm a handful. Yet Dad was a pain in the ass, but he and Mom always made it work."

That was a lot to absorb. Steve wasn't used to Tony being candid about anything. Ever. "You know, I'm glad Howard got married," Steve said. "I only knew him when he was young and single."

He'd meant well, but immediately he saw that Tony was taking it the wrong way. "Oh really? You two knew each other? He never mentioned that. Maybe only a thousand times. God, I hated you."

"I don't mean to make things difficult," Steve said. He wanted to make peace between them. The world needed the Avengers united.

"I know. Because you're a very polite person."

"If I see a situation pointed south, I can't ignore it," Steve said. "Sometimes I wish I could."

"No, you don't."

Steve cracked a smile and admitted Tony was right. "No, I don't."

Tony put on his coat. "Sometimes...sometimes I want to punch you in your perfect teeth. But I don't want to see you gone. We need you, Cap. So far nothing's happened that can't be undone. Please..." He nodded at the pens. "Sign. We can make the last twenty-four hours legit. Barnes gets transferred to an American psych center instead of a Wakandan prison."

Steve picked up one of the pens. "I'm not saying it's impossible," he said, "but there would have to be safeguards."

"Sure." Tony nodded. "Once we put out the PR fire, these documents can be amended. I filed a motion to have you and Wanda reinstated."

Reinstated? What did that mean? "Wanda? What about Wanda?"

"She's fine. She's confined in a compound currently. Vision's keeping her company."

Vision, who had signed the accords, keeping watch over Wanda, who had not yet decided. That was what Tony called keeping her company? Now Steve was really frustrated again. "Every time. Every time I think you're seeing things the right way..."

Tony was genuinely perplexed. "What? It's a hundred acres with a lap pool. It's got a screening room. There's worse ways to protect people."

"Protection? Is that how you see this? This is protection? It's internment, Tony."

"She's not a US citizen—"

"Oh, come on, Tony—"

"And they don't grant visas to weapons of mass destruction."

"She's a kid!"

"Give me a break! I'm doing what has to be done...to save us from something worse."

"You keep telling yourself that." Steve put the pen back on the table. "Hate to break up the set."

CHAPTER 14

While Steve was cooling off, Tony and Natasha observed the beginning of Barnes's psychiatric intake interview. "Hello, Mr. Barnes," the psychiatrist, Dr. Broussard, said as he began his evaluation. "Do you mind if I sit?" Bucky said nothing. "Your first name is James?"

At the same time, Steve sat in a temporary office with Sam wondering what would come next. Sharon entered and handed Sam a sheet of paper. "The receipt for your gear."

Sam read it. *"Bird costume?* Come on."

She shrugged. "I didn't write it," she said. Then she did something unexpected. She touched a key on a computer terminal, and the screen in the room lit up with a view of Bucky Barnes.

"I'm not here to judge you," the psychiatrist was saying. "I just want to ask you a few questions."

Steve glanced over at Sharon. He knew he wasn't supposed to be seeing this. She was on his side. "Do you know where you are, James?" the psychiatrist asked. Bucky didn't say anything. "I can't help you if you don't talk to me, James."

After a long pause, Bucky said, "My name is Bucky."

At one of Berlin's main power stations, a van pulled up to the receiving door. Beyond it, huge transformers thrummed with electricity and miles of transmission lines stretched across the city. The driver honked his horn. A clerk came out of the warehouse as the driver opened the back of the van to reveal a large, heavy crate. He and the clerk got it out of the van and set it down outside the door.

"Just sign here," he said to the clerk, holding out his electronic pad.

Now that he knew Sharon would listen to him, Steve asked her a question that had been bothering him. On the video screen above them, the interview with Bucky was still going on. "Why would the task force release this photo to begin with?"

Sharon stated the obvious. "Get the word out, involve as many eyes as we can?"

"Right," Steve said. "It's a good way to flush a guy out of hiding. Set off a bomb, get your picture taken. It got several million people looking for the Winter Soldier."

Sharon could see where he was going. Bucky was one of the best in the world at what he did. Why would he let someone get a picture of him? "You're saying someone framed him to find him."

"Steve, we looked for the guy for two years and found nothing," Sam pointed out.

"We didn't bomb anything. That turns a lot of heads."

Sharon still wasn't sure. "So? That doesn't guarantee that whoever framed him would get a guarantee that we would." There was no way anyone could make sure that drawing him out would ensure Bucky wound up in *their* custody.

She was right. But once he granted the idea that Bucky had been framed, he had to wonder...how else were they all being manipulated? Who wanted to find the Winter Soldier so badly? Steve looked up at the screen, where the questions were still coming. "Yeah."

"Tell me, Bucky," Zemo said. His Dr. Broussard disguise was holding. No one in the facility knew who he really was. "You've seen a great deal, haven't you?"

"I don't want to talk about it."

"You feel that if you open your mouth, the horrors might never stop." Zemo looked down at his phone and saw STATUS: PACKAGE DELIVERED. Everything was falling into place.

He looked back up at Bucky. "Don't worry. We only have to talk about one."

At the power station, the receiving clerk levered the top off the crate. Inside was some kind of machine with lots of wires and what looked like a giant battery in the middle.

Also, it was beeping.

"Hey," he called to the delivery driver. "What is this?"

"I don't know," the driver said.

At that moment, the bomb went off. It was an EMP bomb, designed to emit an electromagnetic pulse that would destroy electronics anywhere within its range. All over Berlin, transformers blew up in showers of sparks. Power went out for ten million people...and one underground security installation where the Winter Soldier was being held prisoner.

Everett Ross spoke nervously into a walkie-talkie as emergency lights came up in the facility. "All right, come on, guys. Get me eyes on Barnes."

"F.R.I.D.A.Y.," Tony said at the same time. She was the

AI who had replaced J.A.R.V.I.S. after the Ultron mess. "Give me the source of that outage."

In the next room, Sharon caught Steve's eye. Both of them had a bad feeling about the timing of this power outage. "Sublevel five, east wing," she said. That was where Bucky was being held.

Steve got moving. In a nearby room, T'Challa looked up and watched him go.

"What is this?" Bucky asked quietly. He had already figured out that the doctor was up to something. Red emergency lights strobed on the doctor's glasses. Bucky needed to get out of this cell. Something bad was about to happen.

"Why don't we discuss your home?" the doctor suggested. "Not Romania. Certainly not Brooklyn, no. I mean, your real home." He opened a red book and began to read the Russian words, just as he had practiced in the hotel room.

Longing.

Rusted.

"Stop," Bucky said. Zemo saw the panic on his face.

Bucky knew what was coming—Zemo could see that—but he wouldn't be able to stop it.

Seventeen.

"Stop," Bucky said again, his voice a hoarse growl. He clenched his metal fist and started to struggle against the manacles.

Daybreak.

Yelling now, Bucky started to break free of the vessel.

Furnace.

Nine.

Benign.

Homecoming.

Bucky had almost hammered through the reinforced wall, screaming with each punch. Zemo read a little faster.

One.

Freight car.

Bucky smashed through the wall and stumbled out. For a long moment, he was still. Then he stood, hands at his sides and eyes empty.

"Soldier?" Zemo asked, still in Russian.

The answer was barely above a whisper. "Ready to comply."

Zemo had waited a long time for this. "Mission report: December sixteenth, 1991."

CHAPTER 15

When Steve got to sublevel 5 in the east wing, he found technicians and guards sprawled, unmoving, all over the place. Sam was right behind him. The psychiatrist lay in the room near the containment cell. It had been broken open. "Help me," the psychiatrist called weakly. "Help?"

Steve hauled him to his feet. "Who are you? What do you want?"

The impostor didn't seem bothered that Steve had seen through his ruse. He smiled. "To see an empire fall," he said...and that was when Bucky charged out of the shadows.

No, it wasn't Bucky. Not anymore.

It was the Winter Soldier.

He got the drop on Sam and knocked him out cold. Then he went after Steve, driving him back with unstoppable punches from that metal arm. If Steve had been able to use his shield, it would have been an even fight. Without it, he didn't have much of a chance. The Winter Soldier drove him back and pinned him to the elevator door. Steve held the metal fist back with both of his own, then the elevator door caved in and Steve toppled backward through it. He banged off the walls of the elevator shaft as he fell away into the darkness below.

Sam came to his senses and saw the fake doctor slinking away around a nearby corner. "Hey," he said. The doctor ran. Sam got to his feet, his head still spinning, and went after him.

On the main level, Everett Ross was issuing orders. "Evacuate all civilians. Give me a perimeter around the building and gunships in the air."

"Please tell me you have a suit," Natasha said to Tony as they passed Ross.

"Sure do," Tony answered. "It's a lovely three-piece, two-button.... I'm an active-duty noncombatant." What did she think, he had extra Iron Man armor stashed in his shoe?

Sharon caught their attention then. "Follow me," she said. She knew where the Winter Soldier was. Downstairs, Sam was chasing after the fake doctor in the darkness of the sublevels.

Tony paused inside a doorway as the Winter Soldier battled through a group of soldiers trying to keep him from escaping. He hadn't told Natasha the whole truth. He did have a little emergency Iron Man tech on him. Tapping the screen of his smartwatch, he transformed it in to an Iron Man gauntlet. He stepped into the room and hit the Winter Soldier with a sonic pulse from it while the repulsor powered up.

The Winter Soldier staggered but didn't go down. Tony fired the repulsor, but that didn't take him down, either. They exchanged a series of punches, Tony mostly dodging, and then the Winter Soldier brought up a gun he must have taken from one of the soldiers. Tony blocked the shot with the gauntlet, looking in shock at Bucky and the gun that would have put him down. The repulsor wasn't going to work after that. He took one last desperate swing at the Winter Soldier, but an elbow and a kick to the stomach left him gasping on the floor across the room.

Natasha and Sharon tried to tag-team him next, each delivering a coordinated flurry of kicks and elbow strikes that connected but didn't slow the Winter Soldier. He slammed Sharon through a table and got his metal hand around Natasha's neck. "You could at least recognize me," she choked out.

T'Challa saved her life then, coming out of nowhere to crash into the Winter Soldier and blitz him with a series of kicks and punches that actually drove him back. He took a solid punch from the metal arm and got up again, wrestling the Winter Soldier into an open stairwell and shoving him over the railing. Then T'Challa jumped down after him, eyes full of cool confidence.

But when he landed in the main lobby with doors in every direction, the Winter Soldier was gone. Outside, Sam had lost the fake doctor, too. He had gone into the crowds.

By the time Steve climbed out of the elevator shaft and burst through the door to the helipad, the Winter Soldier was already lifting off in a stolen chopper. Steve sprinted across the helipad and jumped to grab one of its landing skids. The chopper dipped sideways, and Steve caught the railing that ran along the edge of the roof. He held on, straining every muscle in his body to pull the helicopter back. The Winter Soldier saw he wasn't going to be able to pull away. He slammed the control stick to the left, angling the rotors down toward Steve, who barely dodged them. The rotors chewed into the concrete helipad, and the helicopter crashed back down onto the railing. Steve got to his feet.

The Winter Soldier's metal arm smashed through the cockpit window and grabbed Steve around the throat. Steve braced himself and pulled back but couldn't get free. As they grappled, the shift in weight tipped the helicopter off the edge of the roof. It fell, trailed by pieces of the roof railing, and splashed into the River Spree.

CHAPTER 16

Zemo sat in Berlin's airport listening to a voice mail from his wife. "He asked me again if you're going to be there. I said I wasn't sure. You should've seen his little face. Just try, okay? I'm going to bed. I love you."

He put away the phone. How her voice made his heart ache. He wished he could hear his son's voice, too.

The terminal TVs showed footage of the day's events. "James Barnes, the suspect in the bombing in Vienna, escaped from prison today. Also disappeared are the Avengers Captain Steve Rogers and Sam Wilson...."

Perfect, Zemo thought. Over the sound of the newscast,

he heard the first boarding call for his flight to Moscow and walked toward the gate. From Moscow, he would complete the final stage of his journey.

Berlin was a big city, and that made for lots of good places to hide. Steve and Sam had Bucky shackled in an old warehouse near a railroad siding that looked like it hadn't been used since the end of the Cold War.

Steve was at a back door, keeping an eye out for search parties, when Sam called, "Hey, Cap!"

The Winter Soldier was awake. He looked around, not trying to escape. "Steve," he said.

"Which Bucky am I talking to?"

"Your mom's name is Sarah. You used to wear newspapers in your shoes." Bucky chuckled at the memory.

Good, Steve thought. The shock of the crash had reset Bucky's mind and freed him from the mind control. "You can't read that in a museum," he said.

Sam wasn't quite ready to believe Bucky was back. "Just like that, we're supposed to be cool?" he wondered.

Bucky caught Sam's tone of voice. "What did I do?" he asked. It was clear he was dreading the answer.

"Enough," was all Steve had to say.

"I knew this would happen," Bucky said. Steve felt terrible for him but didn't know how he could make Bucky feel better. "Everything Hydra put inside me is still there. All he had to do was say the words."

"Who was he?" That was the important question. They couldn't start looking for him until they answered it.

"I don't know," Bucky said, his tone just short of despair.

Steve had been trying to go easy on Bucky, but time was getting short. "People are dead. The bombing. The setup. The doctor did all that just to get ten minutes with you. I need you to do better than 'I don't know.'"

Bucky paused. "He wanted to know about Siberia. Where I was kept. He wanted to know exactly where."

"Why would he need to know that?"

Bucky's face was bleak as he answered. "Because I'm not the only Winter Soldier."

Bucky told Cap most of the story. The 1991 mission. The extraction of extra Super-Soldier serum samples from the back of the crashed car. His return to Russia and the brutal experiments. A month later, there was a group of Winter Soldiers. Over the next two decades, they trained together, fought against one another . . . and then one day all turned on the guards . . . except Bucky.

"Who were they?" Steve asked.

"The most elite death squad. More kills than anyone in Hydra history," Bucky said. "And that was before the serum."

"They all turned out like you?"

Bucky shook his head. "Worse."

"The doctor, can he control them?"

"Enough," Bucky said. "He said he wanted to see an empire fall. With these guys, he can do it. They speak thirty languages, can hide in plain sight, infiltrate, assassinate, destabilize. They can take a whole country down in one night. You'd never see them coming."

Sam took Steve aside. "This would have been a lot easier if we could . . ."

"If we call Tony," Steve finished.

That was not what Sam had meant. "Oh, he won't believe us. Even if he did, who knows if the accords will let him help?"

Steve nodded. "We're on our own."

"Maybe not," Sam said. He got back to the original point he'd been trying to make. "I know a guy."

Back at the base in Berlin, Tony and Natasha were meeting with a quietly furious Secretary Ross. They sat while he stood and read them the riot act about their mistakes, finishing up with an elaborate dig about Captain America, Falcon, and the Winter Soldier, all still missing. "And I don't suppose you have any idea where they are."

"We will," Tony answered. He listed the assets involved in the search. "We got the borders covered. Recon's flying twenty-four seven. They'll get a hit. We'll handle it."

"You don't get it, Stark," Ross said. "It's not yours to handle. It's clear you can't be objective. I'm putting special ops on this."

"And what happens when the shooting starts?" Natasha asked. "What? Do you kill Steve Rogers?"

"If we are provoked." Ross didn't seem bothered by the idea. "Barnes would have been eliminated in Romania if it wasn't for Rogers. There are dead people who would be alive now. Feel free to check my math."

Tony thought Ross still didn't understand exactly what he was up against. "All due respect, you're not going to solve this with boys and bullets, Ross. You got to let us bring him in."

"And how will that end any differently from the last time?"

"Because this time I won't be wearing loafers and a silk shirt," Tony said. This time Iron Man would be leading the search. "Seventy-two hours, guaranteed."

"Thirty-six hours," Ross said. He walked toward the door, calling out names as he went. "Barnes. Rogers. Wilson."

"Thank you, sir." When Ross was gone, Tony rubbed his chest. "My left arm is numb. Is that normal?"

Natasha patted him on the shoulder. He wasn't used to taking the kind of beating the Winter Soldier had given him. The whole right side of his face was battered and bloody. "You all right?" The last thing they needed was for Tony's heart problems to come back.

"Always." He paused. "Thirty-six hours, jeez."

"We're seriously understaffed," Natasha observed.

"Oh yeah." Tony had an idea. "It would be great if we had a Hulk right about now. Any shot?"

She shook her head with a smile. "No. You really think he'd be on our side?"

Tony couldn't argue with that. "I know."

"I have an idea," she said.

"Me too." He looked at her, wondering what she was thinking. "Where's yours?"

"Downstairs." Now she was wondering the same thing. "Where's yours?"

CHAPTER 17

Queens, New York

Peter Parker came out of the elevator and nodded to his neighbors as he went into the apartment he shared with his aunt. "Hey, Aunt May," he called as he dropped his keys on the table and took out his earbuds.

"Hey," she called back. "How was school today?"

"Okay. There's this crazy car parked outside...." He froze as he turned to face Aunt May and saw her sitting on the living room couch.

With Tony Stark.

"Oh, Mr. Parker," Stark said.

Tony Stark. Tony Stark! Peter had no idea what to say. Tony Stark was maybe one of his favorite people on the planet. Maybe ever. Engineer, scientist, visionary...all the things Peter wanted to be. Plus there was the whole Avengers thing. "Umm, what—" He stammered and started over. "What are you doing...?" That didn't work. He tried again. "Hey. I'm...I'm Peter."

Stark nodded. "Tony."

"What are...what are you doing here?" It was kind of rude, but Peter was too shocked to think about manners.

"It's about time we met," Stark said. "You've been getting my e-mails, right?"

E-mails? What e-mails? "Right?" Stark said again.

All Peter could do was agree. "Yeah. Yeah. Regarding the..."

"You didn't tell me about the grant," Aunt May said.

"About the grant," Peter echoed. He had zero idea what they were talking about.

"The September Foundation," Stark said. Peter nodded. "Remember when you applied?"

"Yeah?" Peter said.

"I approved," Stark said. "So now we're in business."

"You didn't tell me anything," Aunt May said. "What's up with that? You're keeping secrets from me?"

He could tell she was both proud and a little upset. "Why, I just, I just..." *Come on, Pete. Say something. Anything.* "I just know how much you love surprises, so I thought I would let you know..." He looked back to Stark. "Anyway, what did I apply for?"

"That's what I'm here to hash out," Stark said.

"Okay. Hash—hash out, okay."

"It's so hard for me to believe that she's someone's aunt," Stark said, looking at Peter.

A little embarrassed, but also pleased, May said, "We come in all shapes and sizes, you know."

He held up the snack she'd served him while they were waiting. "This walnut date loaf is exceptional."

"Let me just stop you there," Peter said.

Stark looked back over to him. "Yeah?"

"Has this grant, like, got money involved or whatever? No?"

"Yeah," Stark said. "It's pretty well funded. Look who you're talking to." He turned to Aunt May. "Can I have five minutes with him?"

"Sure," she said.

They went into Peter's bedroom. The first thing Stark

did was pitch the rest of the snack into the trash. "As walnut date loaves go, that wasn't bad." He looked around Peter's room, noting the old computers all jerry-rigged together. "Oh. What do we have here, retro tech, huh? Thrift store?"

"Uh, the garbage actually."

"You're a dumpster diver."

"Yeah, I was..." There wasn't any way to talk about that, and Peter was getting even more nervous with Stark in his room. "Anyway, look. Umm, I definitely did not apply for your grant."

"Ah-ah." Stark held up a finger. "Me first."

"Okay."

"Quick question of the rhetorical variety." He spawned a hologram video from his phone: a red-and-blue-costumed figure swinging past a car and knocking someone to the ground. "That's you, right?"

"Um, no. What do you...what do you...?" *How did he know?* Peter was flat-out terrified now.

"Yeah," Stark said. Another video appeared—the same figure swinging down to block a car that was about to T-bone a bus. "Look at you go. Wow, nice catch! Three thousand pounds. Forty miles an hour. It's not easy." He put the phone away. "You got mad skills."

Peter flailed around for an excuse. "That's all...that's all on YouTube, though, right? I mean that's where you found it. 'Cause you know that's all fake. It's all done on a computer?"

"Mm-hmm," Stark said.

"It's like that video that records..."

"Yeah, yeah, yeah... oh, you mean like those UFOs over Phoenix?"

"Exactly!" Peter said as Stark got a broom handle and poked it up through the hatch leading to the crawl space above the ceiling.

The same red-and-blue costume that was in the video fell out. "What have we here?" Stark said.

Peter caught it before it hit the ground and shoved it onto a closet shelf. He stood in front of it, arms crossed. "Uh... that's a..." He didn't know what to say.

"So. You're this... Spider... ling. Crime-fighting Spider. You're Spider-Boy?"

"S... Spider-Man," Peter corrected him.

"Not in that onesie, you're not," Stark said drily.

"It's not a onesie." Peter blew out a long sigh and crossed the room to his computers. "You won't believe this. I was actually having a real good day today, you know, Mr. Stark? Didn't miss my train. This perfectly good DVD player was just sitting there and... algebra test. Nailed it!"

Stark let him ramble for a moment, then got to the point. "Who else knows? Anybody?"

"Nobody."

"Not even your...unusually attractive aunt?"

"No." That thought frightened Peter all over again. "No, no. No, no. If she knew, she would freak out. And when she freaks out, I freak out."

"You know what I think is really cool?" Stark sat in the room's only chair. "This webbing. Tensile strength is off the charts." He threw a ball of it at Peter—who caught it without looking and then sighed again. Stark had fooled him into showing some of his...some of the things he could do. "Who manufactured them?"

"I did." Peter was proud of it. He might as well get credit for it if Stark already knew everything else.

"Climbing the walls. How are you doing that? Adhesive gloves?"

That was a little more complicated. "It's a long story. I was, uh..." He was about to tell the whole story, the radio-active spider and the rest, because he'd never told anyone and Tony Stark—Tony Stark!—was right there listening.

Then he looked up. Stark had the goggles from Peter's costume up to his face. "Lordy! Can you even see in these?"

"Yes. Yes, I can! I can. I can see in those. Okay?" Peter

took the suit away from Stark and put it away again as he went on. "It's just that...when...whatever happened happened, it's like my senses have been dialed to eleven. There's way too much input, so...they just kind of help me focus."

"You're in dire need of an upgrade," Stark said. "Systemic, top to bottom. Hundred-point restoration. That's why I'm here."

Peter sat on his bed.

"Why are you doing this?" Stark asked. "I gotta know. What's your MO? What gets you out of that twin bed in the morning?"

"Because...because I've been me my whole life, and I've had these powers for six months." Peter knew he wasn't explaining it very well.

"Mm-hm." Stark waited for him to go on.

"I read books, I build computers...and yeah. I would love to play football. But I couldn't then, so I shouldn't now."

"Sure," Stark said. "Because you're different."

"Exactly. But I can't tell anybody that, so I'm not." Peter paused. He didn't want to tell Stark everything. "When you can do the things that I can, but you don't...and then the bad things happen, they happen because of you."

He saw a shadow pass over Stark's face. "So you want

to look out for the little guy," Stark said. "You want to do your part. Make the world a better place. All that, right?"

"Yeah. Yeah, just looking out...for the little guy. That's what it is."

Stark came over to the bed. "I'm going to sit here, so you move the leg." Peter shifted over. "You got a passport?" Stark asked.

"Uh, no. I don't even have a driver's license."

"You ever been to Germany?"

"No."

"Oh, you'll love it," Stark said.

"I can't go to Germany!" Peter said. This was all the definition of *insane*.

Stark looked him in the eye. "Why?"

"I got...homework." Peter knew it sounded ridiculous.

Stark stood up. "All right, I'm going to pretend you didn't say that."

"I'm—I'm being serious!" Peter said. "I can't just drop out of school!"

"Might be a little dangerous," Stark said, like he was thinking out loud. "Better tell Aunt Hottie I'm taking you on a field trip."

That was it. Peter extended one hand and shot a line

of webbing across the room, sticking Stark's hand to the doorframe and also gluing the door shut.

"Don't tell Aunt May," he said, dead serious.

"All right, Spider-Man," Stark said. He looked impressed at seeing what Peter could do. After a moment, he added, "Get me out of this."

"I'm sorry," Peter said. Jeez, he'd just webbed Tony Stark. What a way to make a first impression. "I'll get that."

CHAPTER 18

Wanda and Vision were having a quiet night at the Avengers compound, trying to follow the news from Berlin, when they saw a fireball rising into the sky outside. It was close—on the grounds.

"What is it?" Wanda wondered aloud.

"Stay here, please," Vision said. He phased through the wall and disappeared.

A moment later she sensed a presence. With a twitch of one hand, she lifted a kitchen knife from the cutting board and sent it streaking across the room . . . where it stopped an inch short of Clint Barton's forehead.

"Guess I should have knocked," he said, and pushed it aside.

"Oh my God," Wanda said. She let the knife fall to the floor. "What are you doing here?"

Clint was wearing his full Hawkeye uniform, complete with a compound bow and a quiver full of special-made arrows. He fired two quick arrows, one into the kitchen counter and the other high on one wall nearby. "Disappointing my kids. I'm supposed to go water-skiing. Cap needs our help. Come on." He started for the door, holding Wanda by the hand. He had created the diversion outside to break her out. But where were they going?

"Clint!" Vision called as he phased back into the room. "You should not be here."

"Really? I retired for, what? Like, five minutes?"

Remaining calm as he always did, Vision said, "Please consider the consequences of your actions."

"Okay, they're considered." Vision took another step toward them, and a stasis field flared out from the arrow embedded in the kitchen counter. Vision froze. "Okay, we got to go," Clint said. The field wouldn't hold Vision forever.

He stopped when he noticed Wanda wasn't coming. "It's this way."

"I've caused enough problems," she said.

Trotting back toward her, he said, "You've got to help me, Wanda. Look, you want to mope, you can go to high school. You want to make amends, you get up."

Vision blew the stasis field apart with a blast from his gem. Clint swore and fired an arrow at him. Vision phased part of his body, and the arrow passed through to hit the wall behind him. He effortlessly knocked Clint spinning across the room.

Clint groaned as he got to his feet. "I knew I should have stretched," he said. He snapped out a baton and charged Vision.

It was hopeless. Vision's power to change the density of his body meant Clint's baton strikes either passed right through him or bounced off him with no effect. Eventually, the baton couldn't handle it—it broke on Vision's chest. Vision wrapped an arm around his attacker's neck and calmly said, "Clint, you can't overpower me."

"I know I can't," Clint said. "But she can."

"Vision." A crimson ball of energy hovered between Wanda's hands. "That's enough. Let him go. I'm leaving."

"I can't let you," he said.

The gem in his forehead turned red as she used her powers to take control of it. His arm phased and Clint staggered free. "I'm sorry," Wanda said. She squeezed her hands together, and the floor underneath Vision cracked. She was increasing his density, making him too heavy for the floor to support him.

"If you do this, they will never stop being afraid of you." His eyes never left hers.

"I can't control their fear," she said. "Only my own."

She leaned forward and shoved her hands down, driving the super-dense Vision down through the floors of the Avengers safe house to bury him deep inside the Earth. It hurt her to do this to him, but she could not stand by and let her friends be hunted down. She had to atone for what she had done in Lagos.

Hawkeye looked down into the bottomless shaft. "Come on," he said after a minute. "We've got one more stop."

Back in Berlin, T'Challa was leaving on his own search for Bucky Barnes, and Natasha was trying to convince him not to go. "It's just a matter of time," T'Challa said as he and one of his bodyguards—a shaven-headed woman who glared daggers at Natasha—approached his car. "Our satellites are running facial, biometric, and behavioral pattern scans."

The bodyguard stopped in front of Natasha, who stood in front of the door of T'Challa's car. "Move, or you will be moved," she said.

Natasha didn't move.

"As entertaining as that would be..." T'Challa said. He gave the bodyguard a look and she stepped aside, with one last challenging glance at Natasha.

"You really think you can find him?" Natasha asked.

T'Challa nodded. "Our resources are considerable."

"Yeah," she said. "It took the world seventy years to find Barnes. So you could probably do better than them by half that time."

"You know where they are?" T'Challa asked.

"I know someone who does," she said.

CHAPTER 19

Sharon Carter had agreed to meet Steve at an out-of-the-way bridge underpass in the countryside outside Berlin. "I'm not sure you understand the concept of a get-away car," she said when she got out of her car and saw that Steve was driving an ancient little car that could barely fit its passengers.

"It's low-profile," he said.

"Good," she said. "Because this stuff tends to draw a crowd." Sharon opened her trunk, revealing Sam's Falcon gear and Steve's shield.

Bucky and Sam were back in the car. From the cramped

backseat, Bucky squirmed in the tight confines and said, "Can you move your seat up?"

"No." Sam didn't turn around.

"I owe you again," Steve said to Sharon.

"I'm keeping a list," she said. "You know, he kind of tried to kill me."

"Sorry, I'll put it on the list." Steve paused and got serious. "They're going to come looking for you." Helping the rogue Avengers was going to put an end to whatever career Sharon had. She would be on the run, too.

"I know," she said.

"Thank you, Sharon." They looked at each other for a long moment and then kissed. When they broke the kiss, Steve said, "That was . . ."

"Late," she said.

He grinned.

She took a step back from him. "I should go."

She was right. They had to keep moving. "Okay," Steve said. She got back into her car. Steve glanced over at his car and saw Sam and Bucky nodding their approval from inside.

From Berlin to Leipzig was a pretty short drive, even in a car that struggled to stay at sixty miles an hour. The plan was to meet there and then go after the fake doctor, who had to be heading for the old Russian base in Siberia. Steve pulled into a long-term parking garage at the Leipzig/Halle Airport, a few spaces over from a white van. Clint Barton got out of the van to meet them.

Steve was glad to see his old friend. Well, not that old. Maybe it just felt like they'd known each other forever. "You know I wouldn't have called if I had any other choice."

"Hey, man, you're doing me a favor," Clint said. "Besides...I'm on your team."

Wanda Maximoff got out of the van's passenger seat. Steve nodded at her. She was taking a big chance. "Thanks for having my back," he said.

With a shrug and a glance at Clint, she said, "It was time to get off my ass."

Steve looked around. "About our other recruit..."

"He's ready to go," Clint said, hauling open the van's side door. "I have to put a little coffee in him, but he should be good."

Lying on the floor of the van, Scott Lang started up out of a deep sleep. "What time zone is this?" he asked as he got out and blinked at them. Then he recognized Steve.

"Captain America," he said, like he couldn't believe what he was seeing.

Steve nodded. "Mr. Lang."

They shook hands, and Scott kept shaking. "It's an honor." He looked down. "I'm shaking your hand too long. Wow. This is awesome. Captain America." He looked back at Wanda, happy as a clam. "I know you, too. You're great."

Then he looked back at Steve. "Jeez. Look, I wanted to say, I know you know a lot of super people, so thinks for thanking of me."

Over Steve's shoulder he saw Sam. "Hey, man."

Sam nodded. "What's up?"

"Good to see you." Remembering their last encounter, when he fought Falcon as the miniature Ant-Man, Scott looked uncomfortable. "Look. What happened last time was a—"

Sam waved it away. "It was a great audition, but it'll never happen again."

"Did he tell you what we're up against?" Steve asked Scott.

"Something about some . . . psycho assassins?"

That about summed it up, Steve thought. "We're outside the law on this one. So if you come with us, you're a wanted man."

Scott shrugged. "Yeah, well, what else is new?"

"We should get moving," Bucky said. "I got a chopper lined up."

They heard a voice over the airport loudspeakers echoing through the parking garage. Bucky listened. "They're evacuating the airport," he said.

Steve knew that could only mean one thing. "Stark."

"Stark?" Scott echoed.

That's right, Steve thought. He probably didn't know about the split in the team over the Sokovia Accords.

But they could explain it all later.

"Suit up," Steve said.

CHAPTER 20

Captain America's squad was on the move across the tarmac toward the helicopter when a small projectile streaked down out of the sky and hit it behind the rotors. All its electrical systems shorted out, and, side by side, Iron Man and War Machine dropped down in front of it.

"Wow," Iron Man said. He retracted the faceplate of his helmet. "It's so weird how you run into people at the airport." He turned to War Machine. "Don't you just feel weird?"

"Definitely weird," he agreed.

"Hear me out, Tony," Cap said. "That doctor, the psychiatrist, he's behind all of this."

Black Panther sprang into view, dropping from the top of a hangar to land near Iron Man and War Machine. "Captain," he said.

Steve nodded at him. "Your Highness."

"Anyway," Iron Man said, "Ross gave me thirty-six hours to bring you in. That was twenty-four hours ago. Can you help a brother out?"

"You're after the wrong guy," Steve said.

But the armored Avenger wasn't listening. "Your judgment is askew. Your war buddy killed innocent people yesterday."

"And there are five more Super-Soldiers just like him. I can't let the doctor find them first, Tony. I can't." It wasn't about the Sokovia Accords anymore. It was about doing the right thing. About standing like a tree and saying, *No, you move.*

"Steve." He turned to see Black Widow behind him. "You know what's about to happen." She gave him one last chance. "Do you really want to punch your way out of this one?"

Captain America didn't answer. Iron Man waited as long as he could, then said, "All right, I've run out of patience. Underoos!"

Right on cue, Spider-Man swung down from another hangar rooftop, snagging Cap's shield with a web and reeling it in as he landed on top of the helicopter. While he was flipping overhead, he also bound Cap's hands together with a second glob of webbing.

"Nice job, kid," Iron Man called out.

"Thanks," Spider-Man said. "Well, I could've stuck the landing a little better. It's...just the new suit...Well, it's nothing, Mr. Stark. It's perfect, thank you."

"Yeah, we don't really need to start a conversation," Iron Man said. The kid needed to settle his nerves. He was in the big leagues now.

"Okay. Cap...Captain. Big fan. I'm Spider-Man."

"Yeah, we'll talk about it later," Iron Man said.

Spider-Man couldn't stop quite yet. "Just...Hey, everyone."

"Good job," Iron Man said again, cutting him off. God, he really was just a kid.

"You've been busy," Cap observed. He didn't try to get out of the webbing. The important thing was to face Iron Man and his team, and stay cool while the rest of their plan fell into place.

"And you've been a complete idiot," Iron Man snapped. "Dragging in Clint. Rescuing Wanda from a place she doesn't even want to leave. A safe place. I'm trying to keep...I'm trying to keep you from tearing the Avengers apart." He got emotional at the end of his little speech. It hadn't hit him until right then how much the Avengers meant to him.

But Captain America wasn't backing down. "You did that when you signed," he said.

"All right, I'm done." Iron Man had tried talking. Now he was going to issue some orders. "You're going to turn Barnes over and you're going to come with us. Now! Because it's us!" He paused, and whispered, "Come on."

Cap still didn't move…until he heard Falcon's voice in his ear. "We found it. The Quinjet's in Hangar Five, north runway." Redwing's remote surveillance had come through again.

Cap raised both webbed arms over his head. From an elevated position on the other side of the tarmac, Hawkeye loosed an arrow, which split the webbing and freed Cap's hands. Now it was time. "All right, Lang," he said.

Ant-Man, appropriately ant-size, was on the rim of Cap's shield. Spider-Man looked down, noticing him. "Hey, guys, there's something—"

He didn't get any further. Flashing back to full size, Ant-Man knocked Spider-Man off the helicopter and somersaulted backward to land next to Cap with the shield in his hand. "I believe this is yours, Captain America."

"Oh great," Iron Man said, sighing. So it was going to

be a fight after all. He ran a scan of the area. "All right, there's two on the parking deck. One of them is Maximoff." Iron Man lifted off. "I'm going to grab her. Rhodey, you want to take Cap?"

War Machine also got airborne. His own helmet display spotted other moving bodies. He zeroed in on them. "Got two in the terminal. Wilson and Barnes."

Black Panther took off in that direction. "Barnes is mine!"

"Hey, Mr. Stark, what should I do?" Spider-Man called.

"What we discussed. Keep your distance. Web 'em up."

"Okay, copy that!" Spider-Man shot out webs and swung up into the air. Cap was chasing Black Panther. He laid out T'Challa with a shield throw, then tackled him as he got up. When they were both back on their feet, Captain America stood between T'Challa and the terminal entrance.

"Move, Captain," T'Challa said. "I won't ask a second time."

Elsewhere, Ant-Man found himself face-to-face with Black Widow. "Look, I really don't want to hurt you."

"I wouldn't stress about it," she said. Then, lightning-quick, she hit him where it hurt the most. He doubled over and shrank, holding on to her forearm and twisting her down to the ground. She fired a stinger, which blew him across the tarmac into a parked plane. He hit it hard enough to leave a dent—and a lot of bruises.

Bucky saw Spider-Man crawling fast along the outside of the terminal window. "What was that?"

"Everyone's got a gimmick now," Falcon said. A split second later, Spider-Man crashed through the window and leveled him with a flying kick. He got up just as Bucky was taking a swing with his cybernetic arm. Spider-Man caught it in his palm. Bucky's eyes widened. That took a lot more strength than he would have expected from this kid, who sounded like he was about fourteen.

"You have a metal arm?" Spider-Man was amazed. "That is awesome, dude!"

He didn't have a chance to say more because Falcon hit him hard from the side and, with spread wings, flew up toward the terminal roof. "You have the right to remain silent!" Spider-Man yelled over the noise.

Outside, Iron Man cornered Hawkeye and Scarlet Witch. He hovered hear the parking garage, keeping them out in the open with one palm repulsor aimed and powered up. "Wanda, I think you hurt Vision's feelings," he said.

"You locked me in my room."

"Okay. First, that's an exaggeration. Second, I did it to protect you." Tony could tell from her expression that was the wrong thing to say. He glanced over at Hawkeye. "Hey, Clint."

"Hey, man."

"Clearly, retirement doesn't suit you. Get tired of shooting golf?"

"Well," Clint said, "I played eighteen, I shot eighteen. Just can't seem to miss." He fired an arrow. Iron Man dodged and blew it out of the air.

Feeling pretty satisfied with himself, he smirked inside the helmet. "First time for everything."

Hawkeye smirked right back. "Made you look."

Uh-oh, Iron Man thought. He looked back at the parking structure just as Scarlet Witch pulled dozens of parked cars out of it. They fell like a landslide on him, burying him under a hundred tons of broken steel.

"Multiple contusions detected," F.R.I.D.A.Y. said when the cars had stopped falling.

"Yeah," Iron Man grunted. "I detected that, too."

CHAPTER 21

Spider-Man and Falcon fought an aerial battle throughout the open terminal. Bucky threw a heavy piece of steel at Spider-Man, who caught it and called out, "Hey, buddy, I think you lost this!" When the Winter Soldier peeked out from cover, the steel sheet buried itself in the pillar next to his head.

Falcon came back after him, but Spider-Man webbed up his wings and he crashed through a kiosk. As Falcon tried to get up, Spider-Man quickly webbed both of his hands to the railing behind him. Then he couldn't help himself. He was too curious. "Are those wings carbon fiber?"

Sam, astonished, had questions of his own. He looked at the webbing. "Is this stuff coming out of you?"

Spider-Man was still talking, a full nerd rush. "That would explain the rigidity-flexibility ratio, which, gotta say, that's awesome, man."

"I don't know if you've been in a fight before, but there's usually not this much talking," Falcon said.

"All right, sorry, my bad." Spider-Man saw Bucky coming out of cover to help. He plowed into both of them, knocking them down to the baggage-claim level. Quickly, he webbed Bucky's metal arm to the floor and stuck Falcon's arms to his sides.

"Guys, look," he said. "I'd love to keep this up, but I've only got one job here today, and I gotta impress Mr. Stark, so I'm really sorry."

Whatever else he was going to do, Spider-Man never got the chance. Redwing shot into view and caught Spider-Man, dragging him by his own webs through the window and out into the open air. *"Aaaahhhh!"* he shouted as he disappeared.

Lying on the floor, Bucky said, "You couldn't have done that earlier?"

Falcon paused. "I hate you."

Outside, Captain America was facing not just Black Panther, but War Machine and Black Widow as well. Ant-Man ran up next to him, all excited with a new idea. "Captain, heads up!" He showed Steve a tiny model-size tanker truck. "Throw it at this," he said, holding a blue glowing disk in his other hand.

Ant-Man threw the disk. "Now!"

Cap threw the toy truck. When it pinged off the blue disk, there was a whoosh of displaced air and it was suddenly full-size...and bearing right down on War Machine.

"Oh, come on!" he said, just as the truck hit in front of him and plowed over him. It burst into a huge fireball, knocking Black Panther and Black Widow sprawling.

"Oh man," Ant-Man said from the other side of the tarmac. "I thought it was a water truck. Uh...sorry."

He and Cap took off running.

Battered and singed, War Machine stood up and glared.

"Is this part of the plan?" Natasha asked as Iron Man helped her to her feet.

"Well, my plan was to go easy on them," he answered. "You want to switch it up?"

Cap, Falcon, and Bucky came together with Hawkeye, Ant-Man, and Scarlet Witch, running in a group toward Hangar Five. "There's our ride," Hawkeye said.

Cap waved. "Come on!"

A searing yellow beam from above carved a trench around them. They froze and looked up to see Vision, floating perhaps ten feet in the air between them and the Quinjet they were hoping to fly out of there. "Captain Rogers, I know you believe what you're doing is right." Vision, as always, kept his tone level and polite. "But for the collective good, you must surrender now."

The rest of the pro-accords team gathered near him: Black Panther, Iron Man, Black Widow, Spider-Man, and War Machine.

It was a standoff.

"What do we do, Cap?" Falcon asked.

Cap kept his eyes forward. "We fight." He started walking forward, and the rogue heroes moved with him.

On the other side, Iron Man's team matched their steady advance. "This isn't going to end well," Black Widow said.

"They're not stopping," Spider-Man said nervously.

Iron Man kept the pace. "Neither are we."

The teams crashed together in a free-for-all, separating into smaller groups and one-on-one fights that swirled back together. The only exception was Black Panther, who had a single goal: going after Bucky Barnes.

Nearby, Hawkeye and Black Widow grappled. When Hawkeye got the upper hand, he had to pause, his bow across her neck. "We're still friends, right?" she said.

He considered this. "Depends on how hard you hit me."

She sucker-punched him. Pivoting into a kick, she would have knocked him out cold—if Scarlet Witch hadn't frozen the kick in place with a flare of scarlet energy. She flicked her wrist, and Black Widow flew away to crash down on the other side of the tarmac.

As Hawkeye stood, Scarlet Witch glared at him. "You're pulling your punches."

Locked in a wrestler's grip face-to-face, Black Panther and Bucky tested each other's strength. "I didn't kill your father," Bucky said.

Black Panther had only one question. "Then why did you run?"

There was no answer to that. Bucky knew he wouldn't understand. He kept fighting, but he was trying not to hurt Black Panther, even though Black Panther was definitely trying to hurt him. His claws slashed across Bucky's metal arm, leaving gouges.

Scarlet Witch came to the rescue again, stopping Black Panther just short of a killing blow and using her telekinesis to throw Black Panther through a jet bridge and into the terminal.

Spider-Man was swinging above the fray, waiting for the right time to jump in and make a difference, when Captain America's shield severed his web. He tumbled up a cargo ramp as the shield came back to Cap. "That thing does not obey the laws of physics at all," Spider-Man said.

"Look, kid," Captain America said. "There's a lot going on here that you don't understand." He didn't want the kid to get hurt for the wrong reasons.

"Mr. Stark said you'd say that. He also said to go for your legs." Spider-Man snapped out a web and hauled

Cap's legs out from under him. He hit the ground hard, got up, and found both of his hands suddenly caught in webs. The kid was fast—and good—but he wasn't a pro yet. Captain America flexed and suddenly pulled the kid off his feet, using his own webs to toss him away.

But he was better than Steve had expected. He hit a wall, bounced off, and swung himself up onto the roof of a jet bridge.

"Did Stark tell you anything else?" Cap asked.

"That you're wrong. You think you're right. And that makes you dangerous." Now the kid was serious.

"I guess he had a point," Cap said.

Spider-Man came after him again, but Cap knew his moves now. He saw the swinging kick coming, and he belted the kid back with his shield, smashing him into the jet bridge's wheel assembly. The kid rolled under the jet bridge and Steve threw the shield to break off the assembly the rest of the way. The jet bridge fell down on the kid, who got both hands under it and held it in place. Barely.

"You got heart, kid. Where're you from?"

"Queens." Spider-Man's voice strained with the effort of holding up the jet bridge.

Cap nodded with a grin. "Brooklyn," he said, and ran to rejoin the fight.

Falcon was having trouble getting away from Iron Man. "Clint, can you get him off me?"

Sighting down the shaft of an arrow a few hundred yards away, Clint said, "Buckled in?"

He was talking to the now-tiny Ant-Man, who rode on the arrowhead. "Yeah. I'm good, Arrow-Guy," Lang said.

Clint shot the arrow, and it split into several homing warheads. Iron Man paused in midair to blast them apart, but that gave Ant-Man enough time to land on his armor without his noticing. He scampered over the metal-clad shoulder, looking for a seam.

A moment later, as Iron Man was lining up his repulsors on Clint, they flickered and went out. "F.R.I.D.A.Y.?" *What is going on?*

"We have some weapons systems offline," she said.

"We what?" *How?*

Inside the Iron Man armor, Ant-Man was busy ripping out every wire he could get his hands on. "Oh, you're gonna have to take this into the shop," he said.

As different systems shorted out and the suit struggled to stay airborne, Iron Man said, "Who's speaking?"

"It's your conscience. We don't talk a lot these days."

"F.R.I.D.A.Y.?" He had an idea, but she got there before he did.

"Deploying fire suppression systems," she said.

Tony heard the miniature invader—must have been Ant-Man, who else?—say, "Uh-oh. Oh boy."

A second later, the fire-control gas jetted out of gaps in the Iron Man armor—and so did Ant-Man, falling toward the ground.

CHAPTER 22

Captain America and Bucky came together near the Quinjet. "We got to go," Bucky said urgently. "That guy's probably in Siberia by now."

Cap looked up. "We got to draw out the fliers. I'll take Vision. You get to the jet."

"No, you get to the jet!" Falcon shouted. "Both of you! The rest of us aren't getting out of here." Captain America paused.

"As much as I hate to admit it," Hawkeye added, "if we're gonna win this one, some of us might have to lose it. This isn't the real fight, Steve."

Cap hated it, but he knew Falcon was right. "All right, Sam, what's the plan?"

"We need a diversion. Something big."

Ant-Man piped up. "I got something kind of big, but I can't hold it very long. On my signal, run. And if I tear myself in half, don't come back for me."

Bucky looked confused. "He's going to tear himself in half? You're sure about this guy?"

Half an inch tall, Ant-Man ran along the cargo ramp where he'd landed after falling out of Iron Man's suit. "I do it all the time. I mean once . . . in a lab. And I passed out."

He leaped off the ramp and landed on the passing War Machine. With the wind roaring around him, Ant-Man touched the blue stud on his forearm control screen. Just like Hank Pym had shown him with the original disks, blue meant large and red meant small. Essentially, he had figured out how to grow as well as shrink. Except it didn't always work. But now was the time to give it a try, right?

Absolutely.

He touched the panel and couldn't help but start yelling as his body expanded from its normal just-shy-of-six feet to something closer to maybe fifty feet tall. He couldn't get much bigger without starting to lose control of his limbs, and even at this size, he was slow. But it sure did make an impression. He reached out and caught War Machine in his left hand.

"Okay, tiny dude is big now. He's big now," said War Machine. Spider-Man stood gawking in amazement below.

"I guess that's the signal," Cap said. He and Bucky made their break for the Quinjet as Falcon shouted, "Way to go, Tic Tac!"

"Give me back my Rhodey," Iron Man growled. Falcon hit him from the side, and they spun away into the air fighting.

Ant-Man, now more like Giant-Man, tossed War Machine away across the airport. "I got him!" Spider-Man shouted. He caught War Machine with a web and slowed him down enough that he could get his balance. Giant-Man stomped through the airport, kicking a bus at Vision and Black Panther, tearing a wing off a jet, and narrowly missing Iron Man with it.

"Okay. Anybody on our side hiding any shocking and fantastic abilities they'd like to disclose, I'm open to suggestion," Iron Man said.

Giant-Man cut Black Panther off before he could get to the Quinjet hangar. "You want to get to them? You got to go through me."

Explosions blossomed around his head and shoulders as War Machine came in firing. Spider-Man tried to wrap up one of his arms and keep him occupied. Below, Hawkeye fired arrow after arrow at Black Panther, holding him off until a final explosive arrow went off in T'Challa's face without even fazing him.

"We haven't met yet," Hawkeye said. "I'm Clint."

"I don't care," T'Challa said. Hawkeye flicked his wrist, and his bow straightened out into a fighting staff. So that's how it was going to be.

Giant-Man kept rampaging through the airport, keeping Iron Man and War Machine busy...but then Vision phased through him, stopping him in his tracks. He twitched and shook himself. "Something just flew in me!"

Passing out the other side, Vision used the power of his gem to cut through the base of the air-traffic control tower. It fell toward the hangar entrance—but Scarlet Witch held it in place, just high enough so that Cap and Bucky might be able to get under it.

Then War Machine hit her with a sonic blast and made her lose her concentration. The tower fell, pelting Cap and Bucky with debris...but they were through!

And inside, waiting by the Quinjet, was Black Widow. "You're not going to stop?"

"You know I can't," Captain America said.

She nodded. "I'm going to regret this." She raised one hand and fired a stinger—past Cap, where it staggered Black Panther.

"Go," she said. T'Challa kept coming, and she stung him again.

Outside, Giant-Man was still swiping at Spider-Man, who was too quick for him. "Hey, guys," Spider-Man shouted as he ran along the top of a parked jet. "You ever see that really old movie? *Empire Strikes Back*?"

"Tony, how old is this guy?" War Machine asked.

"I don't know. I didn't carbon-date him. He's on the young side."

Spider-Man kept going with his idea as he shot a long loop of web around Giant-Man's shoulders. "You know that part when they're on the snow planet? With the walking thingies?"

Of course they did. Everyone knew that scene.

"Maybe the kid's onto something," Iron Man said.

Spider-Man was swinging in tight loops around Giant-Man, now all the way down to his knees.

"I know. Tony, go high!" War Machine said. The two of them drove into Giant-Man's wall-size chin, knocking him off balance. With his legs tangled, all he could do was fall flat on his back with a crash that shook nearby buildings.

"Yes!" Spider-Man shouted. "That was awesome!"

Just as he said it, a flailing swipe from Giant-Man's giant hand smashed into him. He tumbled head over heels, crashing through a stack of shipping crates and lying still.

Giant-Man lay on his back. He touched the thumb stud to return himself to normal size and he wanted to get up, but he couldn't quite make his limbs work. "Does anyone have any orange slices?" he groaned.

Iron Man landed next to Spider-Man and tapped his shoulder. "Kid, you all right?"

Spider-Man flailed. "Hey! Get off me!" Then he saw who it was. "Oh. Hey, man. Yeah. That was scary."

"Yeah," Iron Man said. "You're done. All right?"

"What? No, I'm good. I'm fine."

"Stay down," Iron Man ordered.

"No, it's good. I gotta get him back!"

They didn't have time for this. "You're going home

or I'll call Aunt May! You're done!" Then he took off to rejoin the battle, leaving Spider-Man trying to get up off the concrete.

"Wait. Mr. Stark, wait! I'm not done, I'm not..." Peter had almost gotten himself to his feet, but now he stopped. He was starting to realize he was going to be very, very sore in the morning. "Okay, I'm done," he said.

In Hangar Five, Black Widow had bought Cap and Bucky just enough time to power up the Quinjet and take off. Still rattled from Black Widow's stingers, T'Challa made a last desperate leap for the Quinjet. His claws caught in one of the tires, but he couldn't hold on as the landing gear retracted. The Quinjet sped up into the sky...with War Machine on its trail.

Facing the furious Black Panther, Black Widow held her ground. "I said that I'd help you find him, not catch him," she said. "There is a difference."

Outside, Vision landed next to the battered Scarlet Witch. "I'm sorry," he said.

"Me too." They both knew what would come next. Separation. Prison for her.

"It's as I said," Vision lamented. "Catastrophe."

In the air, War Machine and Iron Man were closing in on the Quinjet. Behind them, coming up fast, was Falcon. "Vision, I got a bandit on my six," War Machine said. When Vision didn't answer right away, he got more urgent. "Vision, do you copy? Target his thrusters, turn him into a glider."

Vision looked up from Wanda and sighted Falcon's jet pack. He unleashed a lancing beam of yellow energy from the gem. Falcon dodged it, and the beam raked the front of War Machine's armor. It destroyed the arc reactor powering the suit, and all War Machine's systems went dark. The suit fell from the sky.

"Rhodey?" Iron Man and Falcon both saw what had happened. Their fight was forgotten, and they both dove hard after War Machine.

Inside the tumbling War Machine armor, Rhodey's voice was tight with fear. "Tony, I'm flying a dead stick."

"Rhodes!" Tony rocketed down after the plummeting suit, but he didn't get there in time. War Machine hit the ground hard enough to dig himself a small crater. Dirt and uprooted plants sprayed out over the field around him.

Iron Man braked to a landing next to the suit and dropped to his knees, ripping off the faceplate so he could see his friend. Rhodey's eyes were closed and there was blood on his face. "Read vitals," Tony commanded F.R.I.D.A.Y.

"Heartbeat detected," she answered. At least he was alive. "Emergency medical is on its way."

Falcon landed a few feet away. He knew it looked bad. He'd never meant for it to happen. All he'd done was get out of the way.

"I'm sorry," he said. Rhodey was his friend.

Without even looking at him, Tony blasted Falcon into unconsciousness with a repulsor.

The next morning, Zemo stood in a warm office on the edge of the snowy Siberian frontier. Before he embarked on the last stage of his trip to the abandoned base, there was one more thing he had to do. He dialed the number of his hotel back in Berlin and heard the familiar voice of the desk maid. "Good morning, Frau Leber," he said in German. She greeted him and he ordered his breakfast, just like he had every morning.

This was the last part of his plan. When Frau Leber knocked on the door with his breakfast and Zemo didn't answer, she would go inside. And when she did, she would find quite a shock waiting for her in the bathtub. After that, it wouldn't be long before the Avengers knew just how completely he had fooled them. Then they would know that even an ordinary man could bring down the mightiest heroes.

CHAPTER 23

The Quinjet streaked low over the Siberian tundra, closer to the base Bucky remembered. Zemo was going there. Both of them knew it...and both of them knew that no matter what, he could not be allowed to get control over the rest of the Winter Soldiers.

He and Steve hadn't spoken much on the flight. Eventually, Bucky asked, "What's gonna happen to your friends?"

"Whatever it is, I'll deal with it," Steve said.

"I don't know if I'm worth all this, Steve."

"What you did all those years...it wasn't you. You didn't have a choice."

Bucky didn't answer for a while. Then he said, "I know. But I did it."

Several time zones west, James Rhodes was going into an MRI machine for more detailed scans on his damaged spine. Tony watched through a glass wall from the next room, looking grim. Vision stood near him, perfectly still, never taking his eyes off Rhodey. "Vision, how did this happen?" Tony asked.

"I became distracted." No excuses, no finger-pointing. Vision knew he had made an error. If he had gone after Sam sooner, Sam wouldn't have been as close to Rhodey....

"I didn't think that was possible," Tony said.

Without changing his expression, Vision said, "Neither did I."

Restless, Tony paced the waiting area. He looked up and saw Natasha in the doorway. Clearly, she wanted to talk to him, and he had a few things he needed to say to her, too. They walked to another part of the facility, where they would have some privacy.

"The doctor said he shattered L4 to S1," Tony said. That

was most of the vertebrae in his lower back. "Extreme laceration in the spinal cord. Probably looking at some form of paralysis." Rhodey hadn't moved his legs since the crash. At the very best, he had bad spinal bruising that would eventually go away. At worst...

"Steve's not going to stop," Natasha said. "If you don't, either, Rhodey's going to be the best-case scenario."

Tony thought she was forgetting the role she had played in the Leipzig operation going south. "You let them go, Nat."

"We played this wrong."

"We?" Tony couldn't believe he was hearing this. "Boy. It must be hard to shake the whole double-agent thing, huh? Sticks in the DNA."

He was trying to get a rise out of her, but she cut right to the heart of the situation. "Are you are incapable of letting go of your ego for one second?"

Tony had no answer for this. They locked eyes for a long moment, and then Tony said, "T'Challa told Ross what you did, so they're coming for you." He was a little surprised she was still here.

She held his gaze a moment longer. "I'm not the one who needs to watch their back," she said.

As she walked away, Tony's smartwatch chirped. A

hologram spawned from its screen. Tony looked at it and wasn't sure what he was seeing. "What am I looking at, F.R.I.D.A.Y.?"

"Priority upload from Berlin police," she said.

A moment later, he figured it out. "Fire up the chopper," he ordered.

Twenty minutes later Tony was on his personal helicopter headed out over the North Atlantic. He knew Ross was at a base out there, and he needed to get this information to Ross immediately. While the chopper flew on autopilot, Tony got a briefing from F.R.I.D.A.Y. "The task force called for a psychiatrist as soon as Barnes was captured. They dispatched Dr. Theo Broussard from Geneva within the hour." She displayed a dossier image of Theo Broussard, who did not resemble the psychiatrist who had interviewed Bucky Barnes. "He was met by this man," F.R.I.D.A.Y. added, and brought up another picture.

That was the guy. They'd had him in Berlin, and he'd gotten away. "Did you run a facial recognition yet?"

Offended, F.R.I.D.A.Y. said, "What do I look like?"

"I don't know. I've been picturing a redhead."

"You must be thinking I'm someone else."

Ouch, Tony thought. "I must be." He needed to program a little less personality into his AIs.

"The fake doctor is actually Colonel Helmut Zemo. Sokovian intelligence. Zemo ran EKO Skorpion, a Sokovian covert kill squad." As she spoke, F.R.I.D.A.Y. flashed a picture of a face Tony recognized. It was the doctor who had interviewed Barnes, no doubt about it.

"So what happened to the real Broussard?"

"He was found dead in a Berlin hotel room," F.R.I.D.A.Y. said. "The police also found a wig and facial prosthesis approximating the appearance of one James Buchanan Barnes."

The whole thing had been an operation to frame Bucky and flush him out into the open. "Get this to Ross," Tony said. Finally, they knew who was behind it all. But they also knew that this one Colonel Zemo had fooled them all... and set them at one another's throats. What would he do next?

When Zemo got to the base, set into a stone ridge deep in arctic Siberia, he had to chisel a foot of ice away from the control panel before he could go in. But the base security system accepted the code from the red book, and twenty minutes after opening the door, Zemo had the mission report he had been seeking for so long: December 16, 1991.

He also found the rest of the Winter Soldiers.

Now the final phase, he thought. *Now all their crimes will be known.*

They would come looking for him. He had to prepare.

"This is the Raft prison control," said a voice over Tony's helicopter intercom. "You are clear for landing, Mr. Stark." Tony stood and let the autopilot handle the descent. He wanted to see the Raft without having to pay attention to flying.

It rose from under the water, a squat black cylinder five hundred feet in diameter, with a few lights shining through the stormy night. Ross had commissioned the Raft for the most dangerous inmates he might have to jail. It was hard to escape when you were in armored cells under twenty-four-hour guard...and several hundred feet underwater.

The chopper landed on a helipad, and the helipad lowered inside. The Raft. Heavy pressure doors sealed over it. Tony got out of the chopper and saw Secretary Ross walking across the landing deck to meet him. *Perfect*, Tony thought. Now they could sort out the truth behind the Vienna bombing. "So, did you get the files? Let's reroute the satellites and start facial scanning for this Zemo guy."

"You seriously think I'm going to listen to you even after that fiasco in Leipzig?" Ross looked incredulous. "You're lucky you're not in one of these cells."

Ross walked away into the base command center. Tony followed, already figuring out ways he could work around Ross. Right now he had to mend fences with the team.

He entered the cell block to sarcastic applause from Clint Barton. "The futurist, gentlemen! The futurist is here! He sees all! He knows what's best for you, whether you like it or not."

"Give me a break, Barton. I had no idea they'd put you in here. Come on."

"Yeah, well, you knew they'd put us somewhere, Tony."

"Yeah. But not some supermax floating ocean pokey. You know, this place is for maniacs. This is a place for ..."

"Criminals?" Clint said, saying the word Tony stumbled on. "*Criminals*, Tony. I think that's the word you're looking for. Right?" He came right up to the bars and pinned Tony with an angry look. "It didn't used to mean me or Sam or Wanda." Clint shrugged. "But here we are."

"'Cause you broke the law," Tony said. "I didn't make you."

"The law. The law." Clint kept repeating that as Tony went on.

"You read it, you broke it."

"The law. The law. The law."

"All right," Tony said. "You're all grown up. You got a wife and kids. I don't understand. Why didn't you think about them before you chose the wrong side?"

"You better watch your back on this guy," Clint called out to Sam and Wanda. "There's a chance he's going to break it."

That was a low blow, Tony thought. But maybe he deserved it. Then Scott Lang joined in. "Hank Pym always said you never can trust a Stark."

Tony looked at him in passing. "Who are you?"

"Come on, man," Scott said. Tony moved on to Sam Wilson. At first Sam wouldn't talk to him. Then he asked, "How's Rhodes?"

"We're flying him to Columbia Medical tomorrow. So...fingers crossed." Tony looked around the cell. "What do you need? They feed you yet?"

Sam looked skeptical. "You're the good cop now?"

"I'm just a guy who needs to know where Steve went."

Sam gave him nothing. "Well, you better go get a badder cop." Tony paused.

"I just knocked the A out of their AV," he said. Without audio, Ross wouldn't know what Tony and the prisoners were talking about. "We've got about thirty seconds before they realize it's not their equipment."

He showed Sam a police picture of the murdered Dr. Broussard. "Just look. Because that is the fellow who was supposed to interrogate Barnes." He saw them understanding what he meant. They had been right all along.

"Clearly, I made a mistake," Tony said, just to be upfront about it. "Sam, I was wrong."

"That's a first."

Okay, Tony thought. *I had that one coming.* "Cap is definitely off the reservation and he's about to need all the help he can get," he said. "We don't know each other very well. You don't have to..."

"Hey. It's all right." Sam thought hard. "Look, I will tell you. But you have to go alone—and as a friend."

"Easy," Tony said. He could do that.

Back in the Raft's command center, Ross was waiting. Tony walked right past him, powering his helicopter up by remote. Ross followed him. "Stark, did he give you anything on Rogers?"

"No." Tony climbed into the helicopter. "I'm going back to the compound instead. But you can call me anytime! I'll put you on hold. I like to watch the line blink."

With that, Tony closed the door and flew up into the cloud cover, far enough away that Ross would be dropping surveillance on him. Then he put the helicopter on a course back to Avengers Tower and jumped out of it as he triggered a new Iron Man armor that he had built specifically for stealth operations. By the time the armor was complete, he was in a full swan dive down into the clouds. The boot thrusters kicked in and Tony turned east, not going back to North America at all.

He was going to Russia.

And he was right about the Raft having dropped surveillance. But what he didn't think of was the idea that someone other than Ross might be watching.

T'Challa lowered his Wakandan aircraft, silent and deadly as an owl, out of the clouds and followed Stark's heat signature. He would follow it to the ends of the earth if needed.

CHAPTER 24

ucky and Captain America saw the Sno-Cat parked outside the base and knew their quarry was already there. It couldn't be anybody else. So this was going to be the final showdown. Steve landed the Quinjet and got his shield. Bucky pulled an assault rifle from the Quinjet's weapons locker.

They stood at the top of the ramp, snow blowing around their feet. Time to go. Bucky had a thought, the kind of random thought people got sometimes when they were about to face great danger. "You remember that time we had to ride back from Rockaway Beach in the back of that freezer truck?"

Cap nodded. "Was that the time we used our train money to buy hot dogs? You blew three bucks trying to win that stuffed bear for a redhead."

"What was her name again?"

"Dolores," Cap said. "You called her Da."

"She's got to be a hundred years old by now," Bucky mused.

Cap clapped Bucky on the shoulder. "So are we, pal."

Together, they went down the ramp and approached the open base door. "He can't have been here more than a few hours," Captain America said.

Bucky nodded. "Long enough to wake them up."

That was the problem. They moved in shoulder-to-shoulder. Just like old times. They walked as quietly as possible down an elevator and followed narrow steel corridors farther into the base. After a few minutes, they heard something behind them. They turned and the noises got louder. A large steel blast door was opening.

"You ready?" Cap said. *Five Winter Soldiers*, he thought. It wouldn't be easy.

Bucky was thinking the same thing. "Yeah."

The doors groaned open—revealing Iron Man. He walked toward them down the narrow hall. Cap stayed on his toes. Bucky kept his gun aimed right at Iron Man's arc reactor, center of mass.

Iron Man opened his faceplate and kept approaching. "You seem a little defensive," he said.

"It's been a long day," Cap said.

"At ease, soldier. I'm not currently after you."

Hard to believe, Steve thought. "Then why are you here?"

"Maybe your story isn't so crazy," Iron Man said. Cap couldn't hide his relief. "Maybe. Ross has no idea I'm here. I'd like to keep it that way. Otherwise, I have to arrest myself."

"Well, that sounds like a lot of paperwork." Cap loosened up a little. "It's good to see you, Tony."

"Me too, Cap." He saw Barnes pointing an assault rifle at him. "Manchurian Candidate, you're killing me. There's a truce here. You can drop it."

Bucky lowered his gun, but he still looked uneasy. Even so, the three of them advanced together.

"I got heat signatures," Iron Man said, his mask back in place as they got close to a larger darkened chamber.

"How many?" Cap asked.

"Uh, one."

Lights came on around them as they entered, and an eerie quiet filled the musky room.

Something was wrong.

CHAPTER 25

The room was filled with stasis chambers, spaced between banks of equipment and instruments. Inside the chambers lay the bodies of the five other Winter Soldiers. "If it's any comfort, they died in their sleep," Zemo said. They could not see him. His voice was coming over a speaker. "Did you really think I wanted more of you? I'm grateful to them, though. They brought you here."

The door slid shut. Captain America flung his shield. It ricocheted away without any effect.

"Please, Captain," Zemo said. "The Soviets built this chamber to withstand the launch blast of UR-100 rockets."

Tony looked at the door, working out his options. "I'm betting I can beat that."

"Oh, I'm sure you could, Mr. Stark. Given time. But then you'll never know why you came." Zemo stepped into view.

"You killed innocent people in Vienna just to bring us here?" *That's what this was all about?* Cap couldn't believe what he was hearing. But Zemo had that look he'd learned to recognize in the war. Something strange about his eyes, an intensity normal people didn't have.

"I thought about nothing else for over a year," Zemo said. "I studied you; I followed you. But now that you are standing here, I just realized..." He was looking closely at Cap's face. "There's a bit of green in the blue of your eyes. How nice to find a flaw."

Flaw? Steve wondered. *Why is that a flaw?* But he had recognized the accent. "You're Sokovian. Is that what this is about?"

Zemo shook his head. "Sokovia was a failed state long before you blew it up. No. I'm here because I made a promise."

Now Steve thought he was beginning to understand. "You lost someone."

"I've lost everyone. And so will you." Zemo touched a

button, and a grainy black-and-white surveillance video started to play on a terminal near the heroes. "An empire toppled by its enemies can rise again," Zemo said. "But one that crumples from within? That's dead...forever."

Cap had no idea what that was supposed to mean. The camera image stabilized on a stretch of road. There was nothing remarkable about it. Trees, a narrow strip of grass on either side. But Tony recognized it immediately, like something he might have conjured out of the system he'd demonstrated at MIT a few days ago. "I know that road," he said. He glanced at the time stamp. 16 DECEMBER 1991.

He knew that date, too.

"What is this?" he asked—just as on the screen, a stylish town car crashed into a tree. A motorcycle curled into view. The rider parked it. "Help my wife. Please," the driver, badly hurt, was saying. It was Howard Stark.

But the man who had shot out the car's tire and made it crash was not there to help. He was there to make sure there were no witnesses. Tony didn't want to watch the rest, but he did, staring at the screen through his Iron Man armor. When it was done, the killer turned to the camera and nodded. It was Bucky Barnes.

Tony stared at the video feed. He'd never felt anything like this combination of grief and rage. The video ended and Iron Man started to go after Bucky. But Steve caught his arm, saying his name. "Tony. Tony."

Tony turned to him, shifting his powerful armor. "Did you know?"

"I didn't know it was him," Steve said.

"Don't lie to me, Rogers! Did you know?"

Steve couldn't lie. "Yes."

For a brief moment, Steve thought Tony might get control over his emotions. But then Iron Man raised his left hand and blew Cap across the room with a repulsor. He went after Bucky with everything he had. Bucky stayed close, trying to stop Iron Man from using his energy weapons. Just when Iron Man got the advantage, Cap knocked him off-balance with his shield.

Iron Man whirled and fired out a device that magnetically locked Cap's ankles together and pinned him to the floor. He spun back to Bucky, spreading one palm wide right in Bucky's face. But he hadn't counted on the strength of Bucky's metal arm. Bucky caught the gauntlet and turned it away. He squeezed it, and the repulsor lens cracked and shorted out. He jerked free, and Iron Man shot a mini missile at him. It missed and set off a small chain reaction that led to a huge fireball in the pipes near the stasis vessels. The fire spread, echoing in the chamber.

Cap finally broke the magnetic band with his shield. The rocket had destabilized the whole structure of huge pipes and girders. It started to lean in and collapse, pinning Iron Man for a moment. "Get out of here!" Cap shouted at Bucky.

Bucky, who remembered the base systems from before, slapped a large button near the back of the room. Far above, a round hatch started to open. Bucky ran toward it and started to climb in a spiral around the outside of the shaft.

Iron Man powered up his boot thrusters and started to follow, but Cap stood in his way. "It wasn't him, Tony. Hydra had control of his mind!"

He didn't care. "Move!"

When Captain America didn't move, Iron Man rocketed past him—but Cap caught his leg. "It wasn't him!" He pounded one boot thruster with his shield. Sparks shot out across the floor. Iron Man kicked free and tried to fly up after Barnes, who was climbing toward the surface.

"Left boot-jet failing," F.R.I.D.A.Y. said. "Flight systems compromised."

But even with his systems failing, Iron Man could fly faster than Bucky could run. He caught up to Bucky and charged his one working repulsor—but Cap came out of nowhere and deflected the blast right back at him. It knocked Tony out of the air, and he fell down to a lower level.

"He's not going to stop," Steve said to Bucky. "Go."

Bucky jumped up to the next level. Iron Man came rocketing after him. As he passed, Cap caught him with a grappling line and jerked him out of the air. They fell together most of the way back down the shaft. Iron Man came up firing and knocked Cap's shield out of his hand. It clanked away down into the darkness.

Then Iron Man spun and sighted the fleeing Bucky Barnes. He had only one thing on his mind. Revenge.

But the computer couldn't lock in on Bucky's form. "Targeting systems inaccurate, boss," F.R.I.D.A.Y. said.

Tony flipped up the Iron Man faceplate. "I'm eyeballing it."

He sighted down his arm and fired another missile—not at Bucky, but at the hinge holding the hatch open. The rocket blew the hinge apart, and the huge steel hatch fell back shut, barely missing Bucky. Now, with Bucky trapped at the top of the shaft, Tony could catch him. He shot upward and got a forearm around Barnes's neck. "Do you even remember them?" he said, his voice trembling with anger.

"I remember all of them," Barnes said.

Even in the midst of his fury, seeing the expression on Barnes's face shocked Tony into a moment of sympathy... but only a moment. His thrusters couldn't hold both their weights and they were sinking back down into the shaft.

Then Cap jumped from a side platform, and all three of them tumbled down, landing hard on a stone platform. Ventilation slots were cut into the side of the wall here, and snow blew in.

"This isn't going to change what happened," Cap said as he got to his feet.

"I don't care," Tony said, his faceplate shifting back into place. It wasn't about principles anymore, or Sokovia or Lagos or anything else. "He killed my mom."

And if Cap was going to defend Bucky, then Cap was his enemy now, too. Iron Man charged, battering him with heavy punches from his powered gauntlets. Cap might have been a Super-Soldier, but he couldn't handle that kind of pounding forever.

Bucky had been stunned by the fall. Now he got to his feet and saw Captain America's shield lying nearby. He scooped it up and ran to help. He knocked Iron Man over with the shield and teamed up with Cap. Together, they hit the Iron Man armor with everything they had, but Tony's anger and pain made him stronger than he'd ever been. He spun away from their team-up and blasted a repulsor right into Steve's midsection, doubling him over. Then he nearly took Bucky out with an energy beam, but Bucky caught his arm and drove him back against the wall. They were both beyond words now, just straining with guttural rage. Bucky dug the fingers of his metal hand into the arc reactor, trying to crumple its housing.

But Tony had one more trick Bucky didn't know about. He unleashed the beam from the arc reactor itself. It had ten times the power of a repulsor blast, and he couldn't do it often, but this was a desperate moment. The chest beam blew Bucky's metal arm off just below the shoulder, leaving a glowing stump. Bucky reeled back and Iron Man hit him with another repulsor blast, overloading everything. Bucky went down and stayed down.

Steve stepped in and just barely stopped Iron Man from killing Bucky, keeping his shield up against the furious repulsor blasts and rocking Tony with counterstrikes of his own. Neither of them was going to stop now.

CHAPTER 26

utside, Zemo listened to a message on his phone. "You should've seen his little face. Just try, okay? I'm going to bed. I love you." His wife's voice. Talking about his tiny son. *All of this was for you*, he thought. *All of it.*

He heard movement behind him and saw the so-called Black Panther, T'Challa, standing there. Helmetless even in the cold. "I almost killed the wrong man," T'Challa said.

Zemo absorbed this. "Hardly an innocent one." He pressed the button to delete the voice message.

So much destruction, T'Challa thought. *And for what?*

What would drive a man to this? "Is this what you wanted?" he asked. "To see them rip each other apart?"

"My father lived outside the city," Zemo said. He was calm. "I thought we would be safe there. My son was excited. He could see Iron Man from the car window. And I told my wife, 'Don't worry. They are fighting in the city. We are miles from harm.' When the dust cleared, and the screaming stopped, it took me two days to find their bodies. My father...still holding my wife and son in his arms. And the Avengers...They went home. I knew I couldn't kill them. More powerful men than me have tried. But if I could get them to kill each other?"

Zemo paused. He didn't consider himself a bad person. He had forced the people of the world to understand what it meant to have people like the Avengers among them. "I'm sorry about your father," he said. "He seemed a good man. With a dutiful son."

T'Challa had no interest in Zemo's sympathy. He had followed Tony Stark here and seen what he and Steve Rogers were now doing to each other. "Vengeance has consumed you," he said. "It's consuming them. I'm done letting it consume me." He retracted his claws. "Justice will come soon enough."

"Tell that to the dead." Zemo thought he could get his

gun up before T'Challa reacted, but he was wrong. Black Panther turned the gun aside and held Zemo immobile in an armlock before Zemo had even seen him move.

"The living," he said, "are not done with you yet."

The fight went on between Iron Man and Captain America. Tony and Steve. Tony kept trying to get to Bucky, and Steve kept getting in the way. "You can't beat him hand to hand," F.R.I.D.A.Y said.

Tony had figured that out himself. He needed some help. "Analyze his fighting pattern."

"Scanning!" He held on, defending, until she had what she needed. "Countermeasures ready."

If Steve was going to side with the man who had killed Tony's parents ... well, that was all he needed to know.

F.R.I.D.A.Y. had analyzed Steve's tendencies, and now she knew what Steve was going to do before Steve did. The fight turned fast after that, and barely a minute later, Steve was down on his hands and knees ... but still blocking the way to Bucky.

"Sorry, Tony," Cap panted, his face bloody. "He's my friend."

"So was I," Tony said. Two more punches laid Steve flat and Tony tossed him out of the way. Bucky lay helpless in the corner.

"Stay down. Final warning."

Steve got to his feet, going on sheer force of will. He remembered the fights when he was a kid and what he'd said then. "I can do this all day."

With incredible reserves, he took everything Tony could dish out—and then Cap got the shield in his hands again. Finally, he had a shot. He knocked Tony down and straddled him, moving fast before Tony could get his bearings. He battered Tony's helmet with the edge, shorting out most of his sensor systems. Then he raised it high one more time, and Tony actually thought Steve was going to finish him off to save his friend.

But instead he brought the edge of the shield down onto the arc reactor, destroying it. With the last of the suit's power, Tony retracted the faceplate. Blood streaked his face, and with the arc reactor disabled, the Iron Man armor was reduced to several hundred pounds of dead weight. Tony could barely get up, let alone fight. Steve staggered to his feet and wrenched the shield free of Tony's armor.

"That shield does not belong to you," Tony said. Steve helped Bucky to his feet and they started walking away. "You don't deserve it! My father made that shield!"

That last sentence got to Steve. He paused. Then, without looking back, he dropped the shield and kept walking. He and Bucky leaned on each other for support.

CHAPTER 27

"Meals at eight and five," Everett Ross said to Zemo later the next day at the Raft. He was letting Zemo know who was boss. Zemo was being held in one of the containment vessels similar to the one the Winter Soldier had bashed his way out of... but Zemo didn't have a cybernetic arm. Or Super-Soldier serum in his veins. Ross thought he would stay where he was. "Toilet privileges twice a day. Raise your voice, zap. Touch the glass, zap. You step out of line, you deal with me. Please, step out of line."

Zemo hadn't responded yet. Ross really wanted to get a rise out of him. "So how's it feel?" he said, trying to needle

Zemo. "Spending all that time, all that effort. And you see it fail so spectacularly."

Now Zemo had a slight smile on his face. He looked up at Ross.

"Did it?" he asked.

Across an ocean, in the Avengers compound, James Rhodes wobbled on the cybernetic leg supports Tony had built for him. They framed Rhodey from the hips down, receiving signals from his brain because his legs no longer could. "That's just a first test," Tony said, even though he knew Rhodey knew that.

"Yeah," Rhodey said. He was working hard, sweating as he tried to control the legs.

"Give me some feedback," Tony said, pacing Rhodey down the rehab track. "Anything you can think of. Shock absorption. Lateral movement. Cup holder?"

"No, I'm thinking about some AC," Rhodey joked. The cybernetic frames were tight around his legs. He slipped and fell as he reached the end of the track.

Tony stooped to help him. "Let's go. I'll give you a hand."

"No," Rhodey said. "Don't. Don't help me." He got himself sitting up and paused before trying to stand again. "One hundred and thirty-eight combat missions. That's how many I've flown, Tony. Every one of them could've been my last, but I flew 'em. The fight needed to be fought. It's the same with these accords. I signed because it was the right thing to do. This is ... this is a bad beat. But it hasn't changed my mind."

That's Rhodey right there, Tony thought. *Never lets his feelings get in the way of what he believes is right.* He reached out and helped Rhodey get to his feet.

A delivery guy, wrinkled and wearing a mustache straight out of the 1970s, knocked on the glass door. "Are you Tony Stank?" he called out.

Tony was about to correct him, but Rhodey burst out laughing. "Yes, this is ... this is Tony Stank!" he chortled when he got his breath. "You're in the right place. Thank you for that!" Glancing at Tony, he added, "I'm never dropping that, by the way." All Tony could do was roll his eyes. Inside, he was glad to see Rhodey dealing with the paralysis so well.

"Table for one, Mr. Stank." Rhodey was whooping now. "Please, by the bathroom."

Tony ignored him. He had noticed that the package was addressed to him in Steve Rogers's handwriting.

When it was time for Rhodey to head back to his room and rest, Tony went to his lab and opened the box. It contained a letter and a prepaid, anonymous cell phone. Tony opened the letter.

Tony,

I'm glad you're back at the compound. I don't like the idea of you rattling around a mansion by yourself. We all need family. The Avengers are yours, maybe more so than mine.

I've been on my own since I was eighteen... I never really fit in anywhere. Even in the army. My faith's in...people, I guess. Individuals. And, I am happy to say, for the most part they haven't let me down. Which is why I can't let them down, either. Locks can be replaced, but maybe they shouldn't.

I know I hurt you, Tony. I guessed I thought by not telling you about your parents, I was sparing you. But...I can see now that I was really sparing myself. And I'm sorry. Hopefully one day you can understand. I wished we'd agree on the accords. I really do. I know you're doing what you believe in.

And that's all any of us can do. That's all any of us should. So, no matter what, I promise you: If you need us, if you need me, I'll be there.

"Priority call from Secretary Ross," F.R.I.D.A.Y. said as Tony was rereading the last lines of the letter. "There's been a breach at the Raft prison."

Ah, Tony thought. It wasn't a coincidence he'd gotten the letter from Steve just now, was it? A breach at the Raft just when the renegade Captain America was sending him a letter that extended an olive branch? *I'll be there*, Steve had written. So would the others, Tony thought. Clint and Lang and Wanda and the others Ross had jailed after the Leipzig fight.

They would be there, all right...but "there" was not going to mean the Raft.

That was fine by Tony. "Yeah," he said to F.R.I.D.A.Y. "Put him through."

Ross's voice burst from the speaker on Tony's desk. "Tony, we have a problem."

"Uh, please hold," Tony said. Just like he'd promised.

"No. Don't—"

Tony put Ross on hold and watched the light blink. He watched it for a long time.

EPILOGUE

"Y ou sure about this?" asked Steve Rogers as Bucky sat on the edge of an examination table in a laboratory built deep in the remotest reaches of the Wakandan jungle. T'Challa stood a few steps off, letting them have their moment as old friends. He did not know either of them well enough to interrupt.

"I can't trust my own mind," Bucky said. The stump of his cybernetic arm was carefully wrapped in a sealant, with tape over it. He leaned back into the stasis capsule, which T'Challa had built specifically for him. T'Challa was as skilled an engineer as Tony Stark. There were thousands of brilliant minds in Wakanda, mostly cut off from the rest of the world—though that would begin to change now. It would be a benefit to both Wakanda and the world. T'Challa only wished it had not taken the Lagos disaster and his father's death to bring it about.

"So," Bucky went on, "until they figure out how to get this stuff out of my head, I think going back under is the best thing... for everybody." The capsule closed and its interior frosted over instantly as he slipped into the frozen stasis.

"Thank you for this," Rogers said quietly.

"Your friend and my father, they are both victims," T'Challa said. "If I can help one of them find peace..."

"You know," Rogers said, "if they find out he's here, they'll come for him."

T'Challa didn't bat an eyelash. He looked out the windows, at the expanse of misty jungle—and at the giant statue of a black panther, a warning to anyone who might threaten Wakanda and awaken the anger of its protector.

"Then let them try," he said.

Seven thousand miles away, Peter Parker lay on his bed and wished Aunt May would leave him alone. But with the black eye he was sporting, she was full of questions and she wasn't letting up.

"So," she said for the tenth time, calling from the kitchen. "Who was it? Who hit you?"

"Some guy," he said. *If she only knew*, he thought.

He scratched at his wrist, where Stark had given him a doodad to help him keep in touch with the other Avengers. "So itchy, man," he said, half to himself.

"What's *some guy's* name?" May wanted to know.

"Uh, Steve."

"Steve? With the overbite?"

"No, no, no. You don't know him. He's from Brooklyn."

She brought him in some ice wrapped in a towel. "Well, I hope you got a few good licks in." That was May. She never wanted him to back down.

"Yeah, I got quite a few in actually." Peter was remembering the giant guy falling down. Man, this hero thing; maybe it wasn't so bad.

"Okay," May said. She still looked concerned, but he could tell she was a bit pleased that he'd stood up for himself.

"His friend was huge. Like, huge." He was enjoying the ice pack. "That's way better. Thank you."

"Okay, tough guy." Aunt May patted his hand and got up.

"Love you, Aunt May," Peter said as she left. "Hey, can you shut the door?"

The door clicked shut, and Peter kept scratching at the wrist device. He touched a button on it, and a narrow beam of red light shot out toward his ceiling. Peter looked up. Spider-Man's face blazed there, just like he was a real hero. He looked at it for a long time, filled with pride at what he'd already done ... and excitement for the future.

Wow, he thought. *A couple of weeks ago I was just a kid with a secret. But now?*

I'm an Avenger.

CHAPTER 1

In a packed auditorium, Lieutenant Colonel James Rhodes, Tony Stark's best friend, stood at the podium and narrated as a film about Tony's life played on a huge screen behind him.

"Tony Stark. Visionary. Genius. American patriot. Even from an early age, the son of legendary weapons developer Howard Stark quickly steals the spotlight with his brilliant and unique mind.

"At age four, he builds his first circuit board.

"At age six, his first engine.

"And at seventeen, he graduates summa cum laude from MIT."

A picture of a smiling young Tony dissolved into a portrait of his father, Howard. Rhodey went on, his tone somber. "Then, the passing of a titan. Howard Stark's lifelong friend and ally, Obadiah Stane, steps in to help fill the gap left by the legendary founder, until, at age twenty-one, the prodigal son returns and is anointed the new CEO of Stark Industries."

Another series of pictures showed Tony's incredible successes at Stark Industries. "With the keys to the kingdom," Rhodey went on, "Tony ushers in a new era for his father's legacy, creating smarter weapons, advanced robotics, satellite targeting. Today, Tony Stark has changed the face of the weapons industry by ensuring freedom and protecting America and her interests around the globe."

Rhodey paused as the slide show ended. "As liaison to Stark Industries," he said, "I've had the unique privilege of serving with a real patriot. He is my friend and he is my great mentor. Ladies and gentlemen," Rhodey finished, pointing off to one side, "this year's Apogee Award winner ... Mr. Tony Stark."

The crowd broke into thunderous applause. A spotlight moved across the stage and landed on ... an empty

chair. The applause quickly faded into surprised mur-
murings.

Rhodey gritted his teeth as Obadiah Stane, Stark
Industries's second-in-command, strode out onto the
stage and took the podium. The spotlight shone on his
shaven head.

"Thank you, Colonel," he said, accepting the award
statuette.

"Thanks for the save," Rhodey said, away from the mi-
crophone so the crowd wouldn't hear.

Stane nodded and stepped to the podium. "This is
beautiful. Thank you," he said. "Thank you all very
much. This is wonderful."

He looked at the statuette for a long moment and then
said, "Well, I'm not Tony Stark. But if I were, I'd tell you
how honored I am and...what a joy it is to receive this
award." He took a deep breath and forced a grin. "The
best thing about Tony is also the worst thing—he's always
working."

Tony was not working. Rhodey found that out right away.
In a nearby casino, Tony sat at a gaming table, betting

enormous amounts of money. He paused and threw the dice, turning up another winner. The crowd around the table cheered.

Tony spotted Rhodey across the casino floor striding toward him. "You are unbelievable," Rhodey said when he reached the table.

"Oh no!" Tony exclaimed. "Did they rope you into this awards thing?"

Rhodey scowled at him. "Nobody roped me into anything. But they said you'd be deeply honored if I presented the award."

"Of course I'd be deeply honored," Tony said. "And it's you. That's great. So when do we do it?"

Rhodey plopped the Apogee Award down on the gaming table. "Here you go."

Tony stared at it, surprised. "There it is," he said. "That was easy." When he saw that Rhodey was still irritated, he got a little more serious. "I'm so sorry."

Rhodey waved the apology away. "Yeah, it's okay."

Tony held up his dice to one of the women next to him at the table. "Give me a hand, will you?" he asked. "Give me a little something-something."

She smiled and blew on the dice for good luck.

Tony held the dice out to Rhodey then. "Okay, you too."

"I don't blow on dice," Rhodey said.

But Tony talked him into making the roll instead. He picked up the dice, shook them, and rolled—but they came up losers. The crowd around the table sighed and glared at Rhodey. Tony didn't seem bothered, though. He collected a huge stack of chips from the table and headed for the door with Rhodey. People gawked and took pictures of him with their cell phones.

"A lot of people would kill to have their name on that award," Rhodey said angrily. "What's wrong with you?"

"Hold that thought," Tony said, and strode toward the restroom. Once inside, he splashed water on his face.

"A thousand people came here tonight to honor you, and you didn't even show up," Rhodey said, following him. "Now you're going into a war zone tomorrow just for an equipment demo. We should be doing that here in Nevada."

Tony sighed. "This system has to be demonstrated under true field conditions."

Just then, the door to the restroom swung open and a woman in her late twenties walked in. Rhodey recognized Virginia "Pepper" Potts, Tony's executive assistant. She wasn't the kind of person who let a MEN'S ROOM sign get in the way of doing her job.

"Tony, you're leaving the country for a week," she said,

following him as he dropped the Apogee Award in the tip basket and went back onto the casino floor. "I just need five minutes of your time."

Before Tony could answer, a young woman holding a digital voice recorder pushed her way through the crowd. "Mr. Stark!" she called. "Christine Everhart, journalist. Can I ask you a few questions?"

"Can I ask you a few back?" Tony replied, slowing down to talk.

"You've been described as the da Vinci of our times," Ms. Everhart said. "What do you say to that?"

"Ridiculous," Tony said. "I don't paint."

"And what do you have to say about your other nickname: the Merchant of Death?"

Tony shrugged. "That's not bad." He sized her up, figuring from her appearance and accent that she was one of those do-gooder journalists who came from a privileged background and had never spent a day in the real world. "Let me guess," he said. "Berkeley?"

"Brown, actually," she said.

"Well," he said, "it's an imperfect world, but it's the only one we've got. The day that weapons are no longer needed to keep the peace, I'll start manufacturing bricks and beams to make hospitals."

"Rehearse that much, Mr. Stark?" Ms. Everhart asked.

"Every night in front of the mirror. But call me Tony."

She frowned. "All I want is a serious answer."

"Okay, here's serious," he said. "My old man had a philosophy: Peace means having a bigger stick than the other guy."

"That's a great line, coming from the guy selling the sticks," she shot back.

Now Tony was starting to lose his patience. "My father helped defeat the Nazis. He worked on the Manhattan Project. A lot of people, including your professors at Brown, would call that being a hero."

She didn't bat an eyelash. "And a lot of people would also call that war profiteering."

"When do you plan to report on the millions of people we've saved by advancing medical technology? Or the millions more we've kept from starving with our intelli-crops? All those breakthroughs came from military funding, honey."

"Did you ever lose an hour of sleep in your whole life?" she asked him. Now her temper was up, too.

Tony winked at her. It was time to defuse the situation.

CHAPTER 2

Tony Stark's home was a sprawling, ultramodern mansion atop a tall bluff on the edge of the Pacific Ocean, with a commanding view of the surf far below. Tony wasn't admiring the view, though. As usual, he was working in the huge laboratory-garage beneath the mansion. This morning, his project was tuning up one of the cars in his collection, an old '32 Ford. He looked up as Pepper entered the workshop.

"Boss," she said, "you still owe me five minutes—"

"Just five?" he asked, cutting in. "We really should

spend more quality time together." He smiled at her, but she merely sighed.

"Focus," she said. "I need to leave on time today."

"Why the rush?" he asked. Tony gazed into her eyes. "You have plans tonight, don't you?"

Pepper lifted her perfect nose just slightly. "I'm allowed to have plans on my birthday."

"It's your birthday again?" Tony said.

"Yep," she replied. "Funny—same day as last year."

"Well, get yourself something nice from me," he said.

"I already did," Pepper said, smiling indulgently. "Thank you, Mr. Stark."

"You're welcome, Ms. Potts."

James Rhodes paced the tarmac. "Where is he?" he grumbled. Behind him, Tony's private jet sat waiting.

Just then, a sports car roared up, a limousine right beside it. Tony's chauffeur, Happy Hogan, popped open the trunk and pulled out Tony's overnight suitcase. Tony hopped out of the car and headed directly toward the jet. "You're good," he said to Happy. "Thought I lost you back there."

"You did," Happy said. "I had to cut across Mulholland."

Rhodey followed Tony to the plane, fuming. "I was standing out there for three hours!"

Tony stopped at the top of the stairs to his plane, a custom-built jet bearing the company slogan: STARK INDUSTRIES—TOMORROW TODAY. "Waiting on you now," he said. "Let's go. Wheels up! Rock and roll!"

Shaking his head, Rhodey followed Tony.

The flight attendant shut the cabin door as Tony and Rhodey settled into the jet's plush leather seats.

After dinner, Rhodey and Tony got into another argument. "You just don't get it," Rhodey said, annoyed. "I don't work for the military because they paid for my education; it's a responsibility to our country."

Tony regarded his friend coolly. "All I said was, with your smarts and your engineering background, you could write your own ticket in the private sector." He flashed a smile. "And working as a civilian," Tony continued, "you wouldn't have to wear that military straitjacket."

"Straitjacket?" Now Rhodey wasn't just annoyed. He was angry. He unbuckled himself and got up to move away from Tony. "You know, the heck with you," Rhodey said. "I'm not talking to you anymore."

One of the flight attendants brought a tray with a bottle and two glasses.

"We're working right now," Rhodey insisted.

But after a while, he wasn't as angry anymore. Tony was Tony; what could you do?

The next morning, they touched down in Bagram Air Force Base in Afghanistan. Once there, a convoy of Humvees took them from the base to a fortified test site in the desert. As Rhodey settled in among the generals and VIPs, Tony went to work. He walked up and down the makeshift stage, boasting the virtues of Stark Industries's latest equipment.

"The age-old question," Tony said, "is whether it's better to be feared or respected. I say, is it too much to ask for both?"

His eyes gleamed as he walked over to a Jericho missile perched atop a mobile launcher.

"With that in mind," Tony continued, "I present the

crown jewel of Stark Industries's Freedom Line of armaments. This is the first missile to incorporate my proprietary Repulsor Technology—or RT, as we like to call it. A breakthrough in energy control and guidance."

He pressed a button on a remote, and the missile streaked into the air. The rocket arced gracefully toward a nearby rocky mountain peak.

"Fire off one of these babies," Tony said, "and I guarantee the enemy is not going to leave their caves. For your consideration...the power of Jericho."

He pointed as the Jericho missile divided from a single weapon into a swarm of minimissiles. The missiles smashed into the nearby peak. With a deafening roar, the mountain exploded into a shower of debris.

Dust washed over Tony and the generals. Tony continued smiling, unfazed by the sudden blast. When the smoke cleared, much of the mountaintop was gone. The generals and Afghan officials nodded and muttered among themselves, impressed.

"Gentlemen," Tony said, "Stark Industries operators are standing by to take your orders." He walked off the stage to where Rhodey stood waiting.

"I think that went well," Tony whispered to his friend.

Rhodey started to say something, but Tony was already answering his satellite videophone. He punched a button and Obadiah Stane's weary face appeared on the screen.

"Obie, what are you doing up so late?" Tony asked.

"I couldn't sleep until I found out how it went," Stane replied. "How did it go?"

Stark grinned. "I think we've got an early Christmas coming."

"Way to go, my boy," Stane replied blearily.

"Why aren't you wearing those pajamas I got you?" Tony asked.

"Good night, Tony," Stane said, and hung up.

Tony passed the phone to Rhodey, and then walked over to a row of soldiers waiting by the group's Humvees. "All right," Tony said, "who wants to ride with me?" Reading the name tag of a young soldier nearby, he asked, "Jimmy?"

Jimmy's young face lit up. "Me?" The two soldiers with him—Ramirez and Pratt, according to their name tags—nodded as well. Tony and the three soldiers piled into the vehicle. Rhodey was about to get in as well, but Tony stopped him.

"I'm sorry," he said. "This is the Fun-Vee. The Hum-Drum-Vee is back there."

The look he got from Rhodey was part bemusement and part irritation. "Nice job," Rhodey said.

Tony accepted the compliment like he deserved it. "See you back at base," he said.

As Rhodey headed for another vehicle, Tony slammed the door shut. Ramirez cranked up the stereo, and their Humvee roared off into the desert.